To look at me, you'd probably think I was pretty ordinary—except for my feet, which are size 9½ M. You wouldn't expect me to get into trouble at school, or wreck little children's minds with dirty books.

For Kate Harris, life in middle school is complicated enough—getting used to new classes, figuring out where to sit in the cafeteria, avoiding kids like Maudie Schmidt.

And then, as part of a school project, Kate innocently reads a picture-book to some first graders and sparks an angry controversy. Is the book "educational" or is it "smut"? Parents, teachers, librarians, and other adults take sides as demands for censorship grow.

In the middle of the uproar stand Kate and her unexpected ally, Maudie, torn between giggles and outrage as they struggle with questions that have no simple answers.

In *Maudie and Me and the Dirty Book*, readers will find the same warm, funny and convincing characterizations that distinguish Betty Miles' previous novels. Beyond that, in this first book about young people's own stake in their freedom to read, they will find a lively, honest, and very timely story.

BY BETTY MILES

A House for Everyone
What Is the World?
Having a Friend
The Cooking Book
A Day of Summer
A Day of Winter
A Day of Autumn
A Day of Spring
Mr. Turtle's Mystery
The Feast on Sullivan Street
Just Think!
Save the Earth
The Real Me
Around and Around—Love
Just the Beginning
All It Takes Is Practice
Looking On
The Trouble With Thirteen
Maudie and Me and the Dirty Book

Maudie and me and the dirty book

* * *

by Betty Miles

Alfred A. Knopf: New York

for Pat Ross

This is a Borzoi Book Published by Alfred A. Knopf, Inc.

Copyright © 1980 by Betty Miles. All rights reserved under Interna-
tional and Pan-American Copyright Conventions. Published in the
United States by Alfred A. Knopf, Inc., New York, and simul-
taneously in Canada by Random House of Canada Limited, Toronto.
Distributed by Random House, Inc., New York.
Manufactured in the United States of America

10 9 8 7 6 5 4 3 2 1

Library of Congress Cataloging in Publication Data
Miles, Betty. Maudie and me and the dirty book.
Summary: Eleven-year-old Kate's ordinary life in a small Massachusetts
town becomes quite extraordinary when she becomes involved with
Maudie Schmidt and an inter-school reading project.
[1. Censorship—Fiction.   2. Prejudices—Fiction.
3. Friendship—Fiction]   I. Title. PZ7.M594Mau
1980 [Fic]   79–19783
ISBN 0–394–84343–6   ISBN 0–394–94343–0 lib. bdg.
Jacket illustration by Patricia Henderson Lincoln

Maudie and
me and the
dirty book

chapter 1

* * *

TO LOOK at me, you'd probably think I was a pretty ordinary person. Except for my feet, which are gross—size 9½, medium. I hate my feet. Whenever I'm in a shoe store I wonder if the salespeople back in the stockroom are laughing at my shoe size. Still, on the whole, I don't think I look that different from any ordinary girl my age, which is eleven and a half—nearly eleven and three-quarters.

And until this winter, nothing much out of the ordinary ever happened to me, unless you count winning the Dental Health essay contest in fourth grade, or my Aunt Lucy (she's really my great-great-great aunt) having her one hundredth birthday last year.

Even my worries were pretty ordinary. Like, who I should be best friends with, and whether certain people liked me. Those things really started bothering me last fall, when I first went to Revere Middle School. Revere takes kids from all four elementary schools in Sussex, so when my class went up there from Emerson School we were suddenly mixed in with a lot of unfamiliar people. Mom kept saying it was an opportunity to make new friends. But it was confusing at first when everyone was sorting themselves out into groups and cliques and wondering which table to sit at in the cafeteria.

I sat mostly with Rosemary and Jackie and other Emerson kids. But sometimes people I didn't know would come around and Jackie, especially, would act more interested in them than me. Right away I'd get self-conscious and blurt out stuff enthusiastically instead of remembering to act cool, the way you're supposed to in sixth grade. Then I'd feel stupid. It didn't help much to know it's ordinary to feel like that.

Then, in January, things started to happen.

First of all, I got excited about a special project my English teacher, Ms. Plotkin, brought up. Without stopping to think, I volunteered for it. That got me involved with a girl called Maudie Schmidt, which I never would have expected to do. Then, the two of us got into some serious trouble. And after that, nothing seemed so ordinary any more.

chapter 2

* * *

MS. PLOTKIN is my best teacher at Revere. She's young and pretty, and she talks to kids as though they were real people. Like, the first day she explained that she'd rather be called "Ms." than "Miss," but right away she said it would be no big deal if we forgot. Actually, everyone just automatically calls her "Ms." now. English has always been my favorite subject, but Ms. Plotkin makes it especially interesting. She brings so many things into it—not just books, but real life.

"Let me tell you about an idea my friend Anne Dwyer and I have been working on," she said that day in January. "Anne teaches first grade at Concord School. She's new this year, too—we met during teacher orientation. Our idea is to start an interschool project in which people from this class would go down to Concord and work with Anne's kids, who are just beginning to learn to read. Anne says that some sixth graders could be a big help in her room, reading aloud to the children, helping them with their own reading, maybe even writing stories for them."

She looked around to see how this was going over. "The idea is that your interest in books and reading would be contagious to the first graders," she explained.

Someone in the back of the room snickered. "Sounds like the chicken pox!"

I thought it sounded neat. For one thing, I've always been good in English. I love to read and write. The Dental Health contest I won was for our whole school district. I got a five-dollar prize and had my picture in the Sussex *Crier*. My dentist, Dr. Klingman, still talks about it when I go for checkups. He calls me "the writer."

And then, I love little kids. I was dying to be a baby-sitter, but there aren't any babies in our neighborhood, and anyway parents always seem to want older kids. But if I could get some real experience with children, they might take me more seriously. Besides, it would be fun to act like a teacher and have little kids look up to me. And it would be interesting to meet Ms. Plotkin's friend. I love to find out personal stuff about teachers, like what TV shows they watch and who their friends are.

So as soon as Ms. Plotkin asked for volunteers, I put my hand up and waved it. "Ms. Plotkin!" I called out, trying to catch her eye. I happened to be sitting in the front of the room, where she had to notice me. I hoped she'd pick Jackie and Rosemary, too. It would be neat if we could all go over to Concord together.

I turned around to make sure they had their hands up, and then my heart just sank. The only other person in the room with her hand raised was Maudie Schmidt!

I didn't know Maudie that well. She hadn't gone to Emerson with me, and she wasn't in my other classes at Revere. Her locker was near mine, but that was all. Still, I didn't have to know her to know I didn't want to get stuck doing anything with her. Maudie was sort of a dope—one of those kids that everybody wants to avoid. It's not that you get together and vote on that kind of thing, but you know. It's hard to explain. There's usually something different about the person, like wearing socks instead of tights or tights instead of socks—whichever's the opposite of what most kids do. Or just being funny-looking in some way. I guess the reason in Maudie's case was that she's a little bit fat. Anyway, I felt horrible to have gotten myself stuck with Maudie. I would have pulled my hand back down except that Ms. Plotkin had already seen it.

"Only Kate and Maudie?" She sounded surprised that just the two of us were interested. "Well, maybe it's good to start small. Other people can join in as the semester goes along." She looked over at the clock. "Oh-oh, we'll have to wait for tomorrow to talk about it, girls. I need to get our assignments straightened out before the bell rings."

I nodded, glad to put it off. I sat in my seat feeling

trapped. My friends were going to laugh at me for getting caught with Maudie like that. I wished I had been more cool instead of volunteering so fast.

Out of the corner of my eye I saw Jackie tear a sheet of paper from her notebook and start to write on it. I knew she was writing me a note. That's a big thing at Revere, writing notes to kids you can talk to in the hall five minutes later. Jackie folded the note into a square and nudged Rosemary, who handed it on to Billy Taylor. The note worked its way across the room to me. Before I even opened it, I knew what it would say.

"You dope," it said. "Now you're stuck with fat Maudie for the whole semester! Why don't you try to get out of it?"

I looked over at Jackie and shrugged, to show I wasn't upset. I was, but I didn't like her to know it. I crumpled up the note and stuffed it in my pocket.

In a way, I guess the note almost convinced me *not* to try to back out. The project sounded good. Why should I change my mind just because Jackie said to? Besides, I was kind of bothered by the way she'd written "fat Maudie." I might have *said* something like that, but I wouldn't have written it down on paper.

As soon as the bell rang, I hurried across the room to go out with Rosemary and Jackie. I wasn't about to start a conversation with Maudie just because by chance we'd volunteered for the same thing.

Jackie began to kid me right away, but I shushed her and pulled her into the hall before Maudie could come up to us.

"Want to go skating later?" I asked, to get on to a different subject.

Rosemary said she couldn't, because of the orthodontist. She goes all the time. She's had her braces practically forever.

Jackie looked funny all of a sudden. "I can't," she mumbled. "I promised to help Mom with something."

I got the feeling she was just saying that. You can usually tell.

I felt awkward all day, between the way Jackie had acted and the problem of avoiding Maudie. At least, Maudie wasn't in any of my other classes. But I was afraid of bumping into her in the hall.

I made it through the day without seeing her, and after school I hung back for a while before I went to my locker so that she wouldn't catch me there. The lockers at Revere are a drag. When I went to mine, the lock stuck and I had to work the combination three different times before it would open. I took out my math book and stuffed my other books on the shelf. There isn't enough room in the lockers for all your stuff. It's worse in winter when you have a heavy parka and everything. It used to be a lot simpler at Emerson—we just had open shelves with coat hooks below them.

There were only a few kids left in the hall, banging their locker doors shut and yelling at each other. I took out my parka and started to pull it on. Then I happened to glance down the hall, and I saw Jackie, talking with a girl called Christine and some other girl

I didn't know. She was acting awfully friendly with them. As I watched, the three of them went out the side door together. That isn't the door you use to go to Jackie's. She was probably going somewhere with those kids. She should have just said so, before. I wouldn't have minded that much.

I stood there looking after them while the last kids straggled over to the front door and pushed out. It makes you feel funny when people go off without you. Sometimes, even though I liked Revere, I wished we hadn't had to go there this year. It was friendlier back at Emerson when we didn't worry about cliques and stuff.

I zipped up my parka, wound my scarf around my neck, and slammed my locker door shut.

"Hi, Kate," someone behind me said.

I turned.

I should have known. It was Maudie Schmidt.

chapter 3

* * *

SHE AND I were practically the only kids left in the hall. In just that short time, the whole school had emptied out. If only I'd hurried! Now I didn't know how to get away.

"Hi, Maudie," I said reluctantly.

Maudie tugged at her locker door. It opened suddenly, and a bunch of books and papers fell to the floor.

"Oh, for Pete's sake." She bent over to stuff them back in, throwing her jacket and scarf out. "I hate these dumb lockers," she said, straightening up. "It was better back at Concord, without them."

I didn't know she'd gone to Concord. No wonder she'd volunteered to go back there.

"At least you could trust people there," she went on.

"You didn't always have to worry about locking everything up."

"I know." I wondered how long I was going to have to stand there with her. I wished she'd push her hair out of her eyes. It bothered me.

"Everything's so different at Revere," Maudie said, as though we were having a conversation.

"Yeah."

"It's as though they expect *you* to be different all of a sudden." Maudie slammed her locker shut and crossed the hall toward me, struggling to push her arm into her jacket. Her scarf trailed from her pocket. "Just because we're in middle school," she said. "There's all this *stuff*—I.D. cards and homerooms and schedules—" She set her books down on the floor and began to yank at her zipper. It seemed to be stuck. She tugged at it, reaching up to push her hair back in an irritated way. "Where to sit at lunch time, who to pass notes to—" She went right on, looking at me seriously.

I looked away, remembering the note in my pocket. I wondered if she could know it was there. "It *is* kind of confusing," I said, not sure what she was getting at. She made me uncomfortable, going on like that when I'd never even spoken to her before.

"Getting crushes on boys," Maudie persisted, as though she was checking off some list. "Talking about parties. Worrying about who's friendly with who. Being in *cliques*." She stopped suddenly, as though she'd come to the end of her list and expected me to tell her mine.

I was embarrassed. "Yeah," I said vaguely. In some

ways I agreed with her, but I would never have said that kind of stuff out loud, even to a friend. It's uncool to talk like that.

I had begun to sweat in my heavy parka. I wanted to get out of there, but Maudie was blocking my way to the door.

She didn't seem to notice she was holding me up. "Ms. Plotkin's idea sounds neat, doesn't it?" she asked, pulling her scarf off the floor and throwing it over her shoulder. She smiled sort of shyly. "I'm glad you said you'd do it. That's why I volunteered, because of you. I figured that way we might get to be friends." She pulled a crumpled mitten from her pocket, stared at it, and stuffed it back in nervously, not looking at me. "I already picked you for someone I'd like to be friends with."

"Oh," I said weakly. Of all the horrible luck—why did she have to pick on *me?* It was so embarrassing to have her practically beg me to be friendly. I kicked myself for not backing out of the project, the way Jackie had said. Now it was too late. There was no way to do it without insulting Maudie. I mean, she had feelings. Just the way she stood there looking at me hopefully with her hair in her eyes made me feel guilty. I knew she'd be hurt if I suddenly said I'd changed my mind. Besides, what reason could I give to Ms. Plotkin? Teachers act like you're prejudiced or something if you try to explain you don't want to work with some particular kid.

Maudie stood there waiting for me to answer.

"Yeah, well, Ms. Plotkin can make *anything* sound

interesting," I said, not very enthusiastically. "Besides, I love little kids."

"Oh, so do I!" said Maudie eagerly. "I have two little sisters, they're two years old and four, and they're so sweet." She smiled almost naturally. "Do you have a sister?"

"No. Just a brother who's older than me—he's in ninth grade." She was practically pulling my life story out of me!

"You're lucky!" she said passionately. "I always wanted a big brother."

"He's a pain sometimes," I said quickly. Boy. Maudie Schmidt was about the most uncool person I'd ever *met*.

"Still—" She looked sort of hurt, as though she thought I'd put her down.

Past her shoulder I saw a janitor coming toward us, pushing a wide broom along the hall. "I better get going," I said. "My mom will wonder." I felt guilty saying that. Mom's almost never home before five.

"Where do you live?" Maudie asked right away.

I couldn't lie about it. "On Turner Road," I told her.

"My house is on Marsh Lane," she said, bending over to pick up her books. "Maybe you could come over someday," she said, looking up hesitantly.

"Sure." I would have agreed to anything, just to get away. It seemed like ages since the after-school bell. My wool scarf was itching my neck. "Well, see you," I said.

"See you," Maudie answered happily. "See you in

English tomorrow." She turned and started off, shifting her books in her arms.

I stood there and watched her trudge down the hall. Her body made a bulky shadow against the light that came through the door. I wondered what it would feel like to be her.

Just then she turned and caught me staring. "See ya," she called once more.

I pushed my shoulder against the heavy side door and went outside. The cold air was a relief. I could hardly believe what had happened. I'd never be able to describe the whole thing to anyone. My friends would laugh, but it hadn't been funny. It was depressing. I felt sorry for myself, but I couldn't keep from feeling sorry for Maudie, too. It must be awful to be so desperate for a friend. I hunched my shoulders against the wind and walked carefully down the icy sidewalk, heading home.

It's ironic that at the time I thought the worst thing about the project would be doing it with Maudie. I had a lot to learn.

chapter 4
* * *

"I DIDN'T know dogs could climb trees," Josh said, looking out the kitchen window with interest.

Automatically, I looked out too. Naturally, there was nothing there but the oak tree trunk. And in the time it took me to catch on and look quickly down at my plate, my last three pieces of orange had vanished.

"Josh!" I yelled, annoyed at myself. I must be the world's most gullible person. I'm the kind of kid who immediately looks down at her feet if someone says her shoelace is untied, without remembering that it's April Fool, or that I have on shoes with no laces.

It was easy for Josh to catch me that morning because my mind was somewhere else. I was worrying about going to Concord School with Maudie Schmidt. Ms. Plotkin had gone on and on the day before about

* 16

how eager Ms. Dwyer was to meet us, and how we wouldn't have to *do* anything the first time, but I still felt nervous about bursting in on a roomful of little kids. And having to walk all the way to Concord with Maudie, on top of it. I'd pretty much managed to avoid her in school, except when we discussed the project with Ms. Plotkin. I'd been careful to get in and out of my locker fast, before she could catch me. But I'd noticed her kind of looking at me in the cafeteria one day, and another time I was sure she was following me down the hall until I ducked into the girls' room and hid in a stall. But this morning I couldn't avoid her. I was worried about what she might say, and how she'd expect me to act. It would be worse than going to Concord with a total stranger to have Maudie Schmidt start treating me like a friend.

Josh swallowed the last of my orange, wiped his hands, and smiled smugly. "Did you happen to notice that your shoelace is untied?" he asked, looking under the table.

I gave him a kick with my stockinged foot. "How dumb do you think I am?" Quickly, before he could answer, I said, "There was another whole orange in the bowl—you could have peeled it for yourself."

"Yeah, but I prefer to let someone else do the work."

"Boy! You ought to get that printed up on a T-shirt: 'I'm Josh Harris—let someone else do the work!'"

Josh bopped my shoulder. "Hey, she's getting fresh." He looked around as Mom and Dad came in. "I might have to report her to the authorities."

"Morning, kids," Mom said. "What's up?"

*17

"Josh just sneaked off with half my orange," I complained.

"Takes after the old man," Dad said calmly, putting two slices of bread into the toaster.

It's true. Josh learned his technique from Dad. Dad just has to *glance* at the ceiling in a curious way, without saying a word, and I'll look up, too, while he sneaks away with the biggest piece of cake or whatever we've been arguing over.

"We may be home quite late tonight," Mom said. "We have clients coming up from Boston to look over the house on Shore Road, and we may stop in to see Aunt Lucy afterward."

Mom and Dad work together. They have their own real estate office in the center of town. They're always pretty busy. A lot of people want to live in Sussex because it's on the ocean, and also fairly historical. The Pilgrims even came here. There are a lot of old houses like ours, but there are pretty many new ones, too, because Sussex has grown up a lot. The Pilgrims would die if they saw the Shore Acres Shopping Mall. Even Dad gets upset. He used to go camping there with his Boy Scout troop when it was marshes and not a parking lot.

Dad and Mom both grew up in Sussex. They were high school sweethearts, which I think is quite romantic. They're related to half the people in town in one way or another. Aunt Lucy is on Dad's side of the family. He was always one of her favorite great-great nephews. That's why we're especially close to her. We visit her pretty often, especially now that she's in the nursing home. She went there after she broke her hip last fall. It's a good nursing home, not like those horrible ones in the newspapers. The people who work there are cheerful and friendly. They make a big fuss over Aunt Lucy, not just because she's a hundred years old, but because they really like her. Josh or I usually go to visit her on Saturdays.

Mom opened the fridge and poked around. "There's some leftover chicken and some salad stuff for supper," she said to me. "Josh, you could make yourself some rice to mix with last night's kidney beans."

Josh won't eat meat or fish because he doesn't believe in killing living things. Most of the time he won't even eat an egg, because it could have become a chicken. I admire Josh for sticking to his beliefs, but it's kind of a drag to have a vegetarian in the family. Not just because of fixing two different meals all the time, but also on account of the guilt. When Josh watches you chew meat, it's hard to forget you're eating animal. It spoils the taste.

"Kate!" Mom said. "Isn't this your day to go to Concord?"

"Yeah." I stirred my cocoa, not wanting to go into it. Mom and Dad were all excited about the project. It turns out that when Dad was on the school board he once heard a talk about older kids teaching younger ones and how much all of them could learn from it, and he'd been very impressed. But as far as he knew, no teachers in Sussex had actually tried it up to now.

"Ms. Plotkin ought to let the board hear about this," he said now. "Get some of you kids over to tell them about her project. With the board behind it, it could become a regular part of the school program."

"Dad!" I said. It's exasperating how enthusiastic my parents will get over anything Josh and I are involved with. "The whole thing's just *started!* It might not even work out!"

"Yeah—wait till the little kids' parents find out what a bad influence their children are being exposed to," Josh said. "A girl who chews gum with her mouth open, talks back to her brother—" He put his dishes in the sink and ducked out of the kitchen.

"Josh, *be nice!*" Mom called after him, laughing. "Be nice" is a family joke. It comes from one time when Mom heard another mother say it in the park. Her kid was hitting a smaller kid on the head with a shovel, and this mother sat there on her bench calling out "Be nice!" in a helpless kind of way.

"I suppose Maudie Schmidt's a good student, too," Mom said, in that generous tone parents use when they're sure their own kid is perfect so they don't mind complimenting someone else's. One trouble with Mom and Dad is that they're so *proud* of Josh and me. I know that's better than if they didn't care or were mean or abused us, but it can be pretty embarrassing. They're always talking about us in this doting way. If a client even asks them about the Sussex schools, they're sure to start explaining how Josh and I get all *A*'s.

"I guess so," I said. "I don't know." Actually, the other day Ms. Plotkin had said she'd told Ms. Dwyer that Maudie and I were both outstanding students. I was surprised when she said it. I wouldn't have guessed. Maudie hardly ever talks in English class, so how would I know? My friends and I usually talk a lot.

"Well, her mother's a lovely person," Mom persisted. "I've met her at Civic Association meetings." She turned to Dad. "Carrie Schmidt, Roy—she worked on the Arts Festival last year."

Dad nodded. "Mrs. Schmidt's a painter herself, I think."

"That's interesting." Mom looked pleased. "I didn't realize that."

I pushed my chair back and took my dishes to the sink, turning the water on hard to slosh them clean. I just knew what was coming—Mom was going to say I should invite Maudie over.

"Katie," Mom said over the running water, "why don't you ask Maudie Schmidt to come over one day? Now that you're involved in this project together. It's a nice opportunity for you to make a new friend. It would be such a pity for you to limit yourself to your old Emerson School pals now that you're at Revere. You want to widen your horizons a bit."

I hate it when Mom says "you want" that way. It's hypocritical. It means *she* wants.

"Be glad that I don't widen my horizons like Josh," I said meaningfully, "and spend all my time at the other end of town!" I was referring to this new girl friend of Josh's, Denise McConnell, who lived down near the harbor. Josh spent practically all his time over there. It didn't have anything to do with the issue of Maudie Schmidt, but I knew Mom was worried about it, and so I threw it in to distract her.

Anyway, the phone rang just then.

"Hello," Mom said into the receiver. She raised her eyebrows and mouthed the word "Miller" at Dad. The Millers are people who bought a house from my parents last year. Every time something goes wrong in it they act as though it's Mom and Dad's fault. Last Christmas Eve they made Dad come over because their furnace wasn't working, and when he got there it turned out they'd run out of oil! And then they expected Dad to call the oil company and talk them into making an emergency delivery.

"Um-hum," Mom said patiently into the phone. "Yes, I understand. Perhaps you should call an electrician. Oh, he won't?" She made a face and pointed to the clock. "Time to go," she whispered to me, covering the receiver with her hand.

I got my things together and called Josh. Mom kept on saying "um-hum" into the phone as we laced up our boots and got into our coats. She waved at us as we went out the door. Dad came out with us to start up the car.

"Give the Millers our regards when you see them," Josh said.

Dad laughed. "Have a good day, kids."

It was starting to snow as we walked down the driveway, dry little flakes, the kind that pile up. Our boots crunched on the packed snow that was already there. In a way, I felt sort of eager to see what it would be like at Concord School. If only it hadn't been for Maudie.

chapter 5

* * *

WHEN I walked into Ms. Plotkin's room with Laura and Jackie, Maudie was standing by the teacher's desk waiting for me. She had on jeans so dark and stiff you could tell they were new, and a navy sweater I hadn't seen her in before. Her hair was clamped back in a barrette. She'd probably made a big effort to look nice. I felt sort of sorry that I hadn't thought of wearing anything special to go to Concord.

Laura nudged me. "Miss Chubby Pre-Teen Queen!" she whispered. I giggled without thinking. I hated to have to go over to Maudie and stand there waiting for Ms. Plotkin while Laura and Jackie sat down with Rosemary and Billy Turner and Steve Bader and started to kid around. Jackie said something to Laura, and they both laughed. I wondered if they were laughing at me.

Maudie didn't seem to notice. "I'm sort of nervous about Concord, are you?" she asked. She didn't look nervous. She looked excited and happy.

"Sort of." I was more nervous about her.

Then Ms. Plotkin bustled in and wrote an excuse slip for us and told us to say "Hi" to Ms. Dwyer for her and rushed us out of the room before I even felt ready to go.

Maudie kept gabbing at me all the way to the office. The secretary smiled at us and took our pass and said, "Have a good time, girls." But as we headed out the office door we bumped into Mr. Staley, the principal, who was coming in.

"Where are *you* going?" he asked sharply. Mr. Staley's a tall thin man with a thin face who always looks as though something's bothering him. "Do you have a pass?"

Maudie said, "We just handed it in. We're going to Concord to visit Ms. Dwyer's class—it's the project with her and Ms. Plotkin?"

She obviously expected him to say something pleasant. So did I. But Mr. Staley frowned.

"Well, go ahead," he said. "Don't dawdle along the way. That's the trouble with these fancy projects, there's too much time wasted coming and going." Abruptly, he went on in.

Maudie and I hurried through the front door without saying anything. When the door swung shut, we looked at each other.

"What was the matter with *him?*" Maudie asked.

"Beats me. He didn't have to get all worked up, as though we were cutting class or something."

We skidded down the walk, making the first tracks in the new snow. It was beginning to come down hard. I was glad to be out in it, even with Maudie. As soon as no one could see us we both bent down and scooped up handfuls of snow and threw them in the air. It's just about irresistible to do that. Maudie packed up a snowball, tossed it at a stop sign, and made a direct hit on the O.

"Hey, good shot!" I threw a snowball after hers. I missed.

"Look out!" Maudie shouted, pointing at a car backing out of the teachers' parking lot. "Someone's coming."

We started walking briskly along to show we were legal, and the car went by without stopping. It's always neat to have a legitimate reason to be out of the building when school's going on. It makes you feel free.

It's about half a mile from Revere to Concord. As we walked, the snow started to pile up softly on trees and cars and garbage-can lids. A snowplow clanked somewhere behind us. It's like a different world when it snows. I didn't have to say much to Maudie. Away from everyone, she didn't actually seem that bad. I began to feel a little more relaxed about her.

When we got to Concord, the people in the office seemed very glad to see her. "Maudie!" the woman at the desk exclaimed. "Welcome back!" A teacher standing at the mailboxes turned and gave her a hug, and the principal, who was working in his office with the door open, looked up and waved. In a way, I wished the project had been at Emerson School so people would have recognized me like that.

Still, it was nice to be in any grade school, looking at things we'd grown out of. Concord was a lot like Emerson. There was the same familiar smell of wet wool and floor disinfectant, and the same little white drinking fountains, and a bulletin-board display called WE LOVE WINTER with exactly the same kind of cut-paper snowflakes we used to make in second grade. Walking down the hall made the years before sixth grade seem very close and yet strangely far away.

We paused outside Room 105, grinned at each other nervously for a second, and went in. There was a sudden hush. Then all the little kids started shouting at once. "Here they are!" "Ms. Dwyer, they're here!" There were so many of them!

Ms. Dwyer was a round-faced, friendly-looking woman wearing corduroy pants. "Welcome to first grade!" she said. "We're so happy you've come." She looked at the children. "Now, then, people, let's quiet down so that our friends can introduce themselves."

"I'm Maudie," Maudie said right away. She didn't act at all shy, the way she did at Revere.

"I'm Kate," I said.

Then all the kids yelled out *their* names. I heard "Myra" and "Thomas" and "Mark" and "Alexandra," but I couldn't tell who belonged to which name. I wondered if I ever would. Even though they were different sizes and colors and sexes, they all seemed to look sort of alike.

Ms. Dwyer asked two of them to hang up our coats. The others gathered around and stared at us. One boy held up his foot and said, "I have new sneakers." Another one said, "We had two turtles, but one died." Then they all began shouting things at once.

"Hey, kids!" Ms. Dwyer said. "Let's make our reading circle."

The children rushed for the chairs and began to push them across the room, bumping into one another and arguing about where "the big girls" would sit. I couldn't believe the noise.

"You'll get used to it," Ms. Dwyer said, laughing. She seemed like a comfortable kind of person. I was sure I would like her. She told us just to relax and get ourselves oriented that day. "Next time," she said, "maybe you'll each bring along a book to read aloud." I couldn't imagine how they'd even *hear* a book, they were so noisy.

But when Ms. Dwyer held up a book and began to read, they settled right down. The book was *Make Way for Ducklings*. It's about these ducks, Mr. and Mrs. Mallard, who hatch their eggs in the middle of Boston and lead their little ducklings to the Boston Public Gardens. Ms. Dwyer probably picked it because the kids would be familiar with Boston. In the book, a policeman stops all the traffic so that the ducklings can walk across the street safely. That's practically all

*27

there is to the story, but the kids loved it. They kept calling out things they knew about ducks, and about Boston.

One little boy was practically falling out of his chair with excitement. When Ms. Dwyer looked up and smiled at him he yelled out, "I have a new puppy!"

That seemed off the subject to me, but Ms. Dwyer stopped her reading to answer him. "That's wonderful, Simon," she said. Then she went on without even losing her place.

Maudie shifted uncomfortably on the little first-grade chair. "I don't see how she reads and listens at the same time," she whispered to me.

"Me, either." I wondered how *I* would be able to do it.

Afterward, Ms. Dwyer helped the children choose their own books to look at. They settled down on the pillows in the reading corner and at tables around the room and began to read quietly. I don't think they were actually reading the words, but they turned pages very seriously. They looked so cute.

Ms. Dwyer pulled a little chair over to us and began to talk about the kids in a thoughtful way. She pointed out things I hadn't even noticed, like which ones had been the most interested in the book and who had been restless. She said she was especially pleased that the boy named Simon had told about his puppy because he was usually so shy.

"If you can just find books that relate to the children's interests," she told us, "they'll often speak up and get involved. It makes them feel more confident about books, and about reading."

Just from the way she talked, I could tell what a good teacher Ms. Dwyer was. She made *me* feel confident when she said we would really be a big help to her and to the kids. She wanted us to work with them individually, too, like tutors. As she was talking, I got an idea. I'd try to bring in a book about dogs, or puppies, the next time, if I could find a good one. Simon would probably like that.

We stayed in the room for about an hour, talking with all the kids and looking at their projects. It was such a pleasant room—there were plants on the windowsill and block buildings on the floor and lots of bright paintings on the bulletin board. And the kids were so cute. The little girl named Myra took my hand and showed me her sweet-potato plant. When it was time for us to go, she ran up and hugged me!

"See you next week," Ms. Dwyer said at the door. "I've enjoyed your visit so much."

I could tell she wasn't just saying that. She really meant it.

Before we left the building, Maudie took me to the library and introduced me to the librarian, Mrs. Brooks. She was a grandmotherly woman who hugged Maudie and told her how much she'd grown. I know she didn't mean anything by that, but Maudie blushed and I felt sort of sorry for her. Mrs. Brooks said we should stop in any time we liked. She also said we should browse in the Sussex library picture-book collection, because it was the biggest in town. That's the library I always go to. It's neat. A sort of second cousin of mine, Gerda Whitman, works there. Mrs. Brooks said she thought the project was a great idea and that we'd be a wonderful influence on the children.

It seemed as though everyone at Concord appreciated us. The principal even came out of his office to say "Hi" to Maudie and introduce himself to me. Mr. Hofsteder. He was a friendly and enthusiastic person, not at all grim like Mr. Staley.

"Thanks for coming!" he said, pumping our hands up and down as though we were important visitors. "You're going to be a real asset."

He made me feel good. The whole visit did. I could tell Maudie was pleased with it, too. All the way back, she talked about how cute the kids were and how much she liked Ms. Dwyer. Her face was flushed with excitement. She skidded through the fresh snow and began singing her old school song, "Oh, Concord School, dear Concord School," in a funny way that made me laugh.

"You must have liked going back," I said.

"Oh, yeah," Maudie said happily. "I loved Concord." Then her face tightened up a little. "I didn't have *that* many friends there," she said. "But in a way our whole class was friendly." She kicked up a clump of snow. "Now everybody's scattered all over Revere, and my best friend from last year moved to New York. So—" She looked at me and shrugged.

I suddenly felt sorry for her. "Want to go to the

library tomorrow and look at books?" I asked. It wouldn't kill me to be nice to her for just the one afternoon. Anyway, it would be more sensible to pick out our books together.

Maudie's face lit up. "Oh, sure! Neat!" she said eagerly. "And then you could come over to my house afterward," she rushed on. Then she caught herself. "That is, if you wanted to."

"Well, sure," I said, carefully leaving myself an out. "If I'm not busy or something."

I should have known it. Just because I'd acted halfway decent to Maudie out of sympathy, she was already probably starting to think I was her *friend*.

chapter 6

* * *

NATURALLY, the next day turned out to be sunny for the first time that week. The sky was that bright winter blue and the snow sparkled in the sunlight. It was a perfect day for skating. Instead, I was walking to the library with Maudie Schmidt.

All my friends were at the pond. They'd planned it at lunch time. Jackie and Laura were meeting at Chris's. Rosemary was going straight to the pond from the dentist's. I was the only one who couldn't go at all.

"Come down when you're finished, then," Jackie had said indifferently when I mumbled something about the library. She sounded as though she didn't care whether I did or not, as long as the others were coming.

"It'll probably be too late," I said, deciding right

then that I might as well go to Maudie's house. She'd brought it up again in the hall that morning, looking so hopeful that I'd been ashamed to say no. I hadn't actually promised, but she was probably counting on it. At least, Maudie *wanted* me.

Jackie had rushed away from the table with Chris and Laura, giggling about which one of them might get into Steve Bader's math work group. Steve Bader's this boy everybody suddenly seemed to have a crush on, I guess because he just came here from California this year and so he seemed more foreign and interesting than boys like Billy Taylor or Cal Berg who've always been around. I actually met Steve first, because his family bought their house through my parents. I knew that his father was a chemist who'd been transferred east and that he had a sister in high school. He turned out to be in three of my classes, and he always said "Hi" and stuff. I never had that much of a conversation with him, but I don't think Chris really did either, although to hear her talk you'd think she owned him.

"Chris acts so crazy sometimes," Rosemary had said, looking after them. "If I were Steve Bader, I'd be embarrassed to have her falling all over me."

"I know it." I picked up my tray and followed Rosemary to the trash containers. Even if I liked some boy, I'd try to be more cool about showing it.

Out of the corner of my eye I saw Maudie waving at me as I dumped my silverware into the bin. She was sitting at one of the tables in the back of the cafeteria where kids who don't have any special table to go to

33

hang out together. I tried to wave back inconspicuously, but Rosemary noticed.

"Hey, I forgot to ask—what was it like when you went down to Concord with Maudie?"

"It was pretty interesting," I said. "The kids are so cute. You should see them, Rosie. Next time we go we have to read them a book. That's why I'm going to the library today—to pick one out." I didn't feel like bringing Maudie into it.

"What's Maudie like?" Rosemary asked anyway.

I made a face. "Actually," I said, to be fair, "she's not that bad, once you get to know her a little. She was pretty nice with the kids. She used to go to Concord."

"She's in science with me," Rosemary said. "She seems O.K." She pulled the cafeteria door open and we went out. "I think it's sort of mean," she went on, "the way some kids make fun of her. I mean, she may be a little fat, but there's nothing *wrong* with her."

"That's what *I* think!" I was glad she said it, even though I was ashamed that it took someone else's opinion to make me feel O.K. about my own.

"She's coming to the library with me today," I added, to make up for not mentioning it before.

The bell rang. "See you tomorrow," Rosemary said.

"O.K." It was funny how just talking to Rosemary had made me feel better. By the time I met Maudie at her locker after school, I was almost looking forward to going to the library with her.

"I'm really glad you're coming over," Maudie said now, as we walked up the path. "I already told Mom you probably would." She tugged nervously at her book bag. "Mom's always bugging me to ask someone, but, you know—" She sort of laughed.

"Mine, too!" Maybe everybody has that problem with mothers. But it was probably worse for Maudie because she wouldn't know who to ask, or whether they'd want to come if she did.

It was nice and warm inside the library. We hung up our things and went downstairs to the children's room. The whole building's only a couple of years old. The library used to be in a big old house with window seats you could curl up on to read. I miss that part, but the new library's neat. One whole side of it is glass and looks out over the marshes. There's a big comfortable couch in the children's room. Gerda Whitman, this relative of mine, came back to work there after she went away to library school. I like her.

Gerda wasn't around when we got downstairs. There were just a couple of little kids sitting there with their mother.

"We have to find really interesting books, to hold their attention," I said loudly to Maudie so that the mother would see we were practically professional. "Their attention span's so short." Ms. Dwyer had said that.

We pulled two chairs over to the picture-book shelves and started to browse through the books.

"Remember *Curious George?*" Maudie asked, taking it down.

"Oh, yeah, I read all those books. They used to crack me up." I found a book called *Umbrella*. "Hey, my teacher read this to us in first grade!"

It's funny how just the look and feel of a book takes you back to when you first read it. Maudie and I sat in front of the bookshelves for a long time, showing each other old favorites and looking at new books we didn't know. After a while the mother and kids left. I still hadn't found a book about dogs that seemed right for Simon.

Then Gerda came in with a stack of books. "Hi, Kate!" she said. "Nice to see you. I thought maybe you'd forsaken us for the Young Adult room."

"Hi, Gerda:" I introduced her to Maudie and explained why we were there.

"Oh, sure," Gerda said right away. "Mrs. Brooks up at Concord was telling me about that, but she didn't mention your names. It sounds like a great idea. Have you picked out your books yet?"

Maudie held out *Little Bear*. "I'd like to read them this one. It's still my favorite. Do you think it would be good?"

"Oh, yes," Gerda said. "I never knew a kid who didn't love it."

"Listen, Gerda," I said. "I'm looking for a book about dogs, or puppies. Do you know one that little kids would like?"

Gerda thought a minute. "Offhand, I can think of a couple. There's *The Big Book of Dogs*, but the pictures aren't that exciting. We have several books on dog training, but they're probably for older kids. Oh, wait—" She bent over the shelves. "What about this?" She handed me a book. "*The Birthday Dog*. It's a pleasant story. The words are easy, and the drawings are very clear and realistic."

The book looked good. It was about a boy named Benjamin who wants a puppy for his birthday. He wishes he could have one that looked like Blackie, the dog next door. She's going to have puppies, but not in time for his birthday. When the day comes, there isn't any puppy with his presents and he's very disappointed until he opens a birthday card that says he's getting one of Blackie's when they're born. A few days later there's a phone call and Benjamin and his father hurry next door just in time to see the first puppy get born. He picks that one for his very own. Day by day he watches it grow, until finally it's big enough to leave its mother. Then he brings it home and names it Happy, for Happy Birthday.

"I bet Simon would love that," Maudie said. "The other kids, too."

"Especially since it's Benjamin's sixth birthday," I said. "That's the same age most of them are. I think I'd like to take this one, Gerda. Thanks."

Gerda stamped our books and told us to be sure to come and tell her how the kids liked them. Then Maudie and I went to the room that has older kids' books and hung around there for a while, checking out the new titles. It turned out that Maudie loves to read, too. We had a lot of the same favorite authors. We each checked out four books for ourselves. Then we got our coats and went out and started walking to Maudie's house. All the way there we talked about books and authors and our best characters. Mine's Julie from *Julie of the Wolves*, because she's so brave. Maudie said hers was Harriet the Spy, because she's so funny.

"Besides," she said hesitantly, "I feel the way Harriet does, sometimes. Even if she's younger. You know—"

"Yeah," I said quickly. I knew what she meant—that Harriet was kind of an outsider, too. It was good Maudie didn't have to come right out and say it in so many words. That's a convenient thing about books. You can talk about them without having to discuss your own feelings, and the other person will understand because they've read the same thing.

I would have thought it would be awkward to walk all the way to Maudie's house with her, making conversation. But I was beginning to feel a lot more comfortable with Maudie.

"Here we are." She stopped in front of a white house with an elm tree in front.

I followed her up the walk. Before we got to the door, her little sisters opened it and held it open wide the way Dad always tells us not to, because it wastes oil. As soon as we went inside, they started jumping on Maudie. They were both very small, but they looked like Maudie. They had wavy blond hair just like hers. One's name was Andrea and the other one was Reenie, for Irene.

"Hey, don't knock me down!" Maudie laughed and untangled herself. "This is Kate," she told the girls. "My friend."

I didn't mind it when she said that. Anyway, to

little kids, anyone you happen to be with is a friend. Maudie's sisters stared at me briefly, and went on shouting news at her.

"Hey, *kids*—shut the door!" Maudie's mother came downstairs. She gave Maudie a hug and smiled at me. "You're Kate. It's nice to meet you. Come on in and take off your things, you look frozen. There's cocoa for you in the kitchen."

I was surprised at the way Mrs. Schmidt looked. She looked a lot like Maudie—she was tall and heavy, with the same kind of hair—but she was beautiful. I wondered if Maudie might turn out to look like that when she got older. Maybe, when she had a figure and all, like her mother.

We went into their kitchen, which was really pretty. It had a polished wood table and chairs, and copper pots hanging from a rack above the stove, and a big oil painting on one wall.

"Oh, I like that painting," I said. It was in my favorite colors, orange and red.

"Do you? I'm glad," Mrs. Schmidt said. "It's mine."

"Mommy's an artist," said Andrea proudly. "I'm going to be an artist, too."

"So'm I," shouted Reenie. "So's Maudie, right, Maudie?"

"I don't know," Maudie said, glancing shyly at me. "I was just thinking how neat it would be to write books for kids."

I'd been thinking that exact same thing!

Maudie's mother wanted to see the books we'd picked, so Maudie went out to the hall to get them.

"Read to us!" Reenie demanded when she brought them back.

But Mrs. Schmidt said the girls should let us go up to Maudie's room and be alone. "How about if *I* read them to you?" she said, hauling Andrea onto her lap and putting an arm around Reenie. "I'm afraid you'll discover that Maudie's room's pretty messy," she said apologetically to me.

"So's mine!" I told her. "Mom says that if I want to live like a pig it's my own business, as long as I keep my bedroom door shut."

Maudie and her mother looked at each other and laughed. "That's what I always tell Maudie," said Mrs. Schmidt comfortably. "Kate, don't let me forget—be sure to tell your mother I said hello." She shifted Andrea on her lap. "I've enjoyed hearing her talk at Arts Council meetings."

"I will, thanks." I thought it was good Mrs. Schmidt didn't try to make a big thing out of knowing Mom, or imply that Maudie and I should be friends just for that reason.

"Come on upstairs." Maudie grabbed my arm.

Her room *was* messy—much worse than mine, actually. I wished Mom could have seen it. Sometimes she acts as though she thinks I'm the only person in the world who doesn't make their bed. Still, Maudie's room was pretty. She had plants hanging down from both windows, and there was a view of the marsh outside them. You could even see a teeny strip of ocean.

Maudie pulled a quilt off the floor and threw it onto her unmade bed. "Here. Sit down."

"Your mom's nice," I said, meaning it. "Your sisters, too."

"Thanks." Maudie smiled suddenly.

There was a top hat hanging on the wall over the bed. "Where'd you get that hat?" I asked.

"At some fair." Maudie took it down and plonked it on her head. "It's my Harpo Marx hat." She did look sort of like Harpo with her hair sticking out from under it.

"Do you like the Marx Brothers?" I asked, laughing at the faces she was making.

"I love them! Did you ever see *A Night at the Opera*?"

"I've seen just about all the movies they ever made," I told her.

"I can do Groucho," Maudie said. She tossed the hat onto her bed, grabbed a pencil, and stuck it in her mouth like a cigar. Then she glided across the room with her knees bent, Groucho style.

"Hey, you're good!" She was really terrific. "I could never get the walk right," I told her.

"It's easy. Just do this"—Maudie pulled me off the bed and pushed me down into a crouch—"and now move!"

I took a bent-knee step. It felt right.

"See? You're doing it!" Maudie jumped in front of me, waving the pencil.

I started copying her movements. Deadpan, we matched steps, taking our cues from each other until our moves reflected each other's almost exactly. Then I stubbed my toe and slid down to the floor, laughing.

"Want to see my Marx Brothers book?" Maudie asked, taking it from her bookshelf. "I have a 'Monty Python,' too, and 'Saturday Night Live.' "

She threw the books on her bed and we started hunting through them for scenes we remembered. It turned out we'd watched a lot of the same movies and television shows. Maudie knew a whole batch of routines by heart. She acted out the Coneheads in such a funny way that I was rolling around on the bed laughing.

Then Maudie's mother called upstairs to say it was six o'clock. The time had gone so fast! Maudie and I put on our coats, and she and Mrs. Schmidt drove me home, with the girls coming along for the ride.

"Here's my house," I said when we got there. "Thanks, Mrs. Schmidt. So long, Reenie and Andrea. Thanks, Maudie. I had a really good time."

"Me, too," Maudie said. "Come again soon." She didn't sound at all hesitant.

"I will," I said, not hesitating either. "Only you should come to my house first."

I stood in front of my house in the dark, watching the car drive off with Maudie's sisters waving against the back window.

I guess that day was the first time we really started being friends.

chapter 7

* * *

GOING TO Concord the second time was a lot different. From the moment we walked in and Mr. Hofsteder looked up from his desk and waved, it felt as though we belonged there. And then, it was different to be comfortable with Maudie. That made me more relaxed. I was a little nervous about reading my book aloud, but I was kind of eager, too. I'd practiced on my family a couple of times. They really liked the book. So did Ms. Plotkin. She said Maudie and I had both made good choices.

"*Little Bear*'s such a warm, loving story," she'd said. "It's nice to read them a book that they'll be able to read for themselves pretty soon. And I bet they'll love *The Birthday Dog*. Kids that age are fascinated by baby animals."

"Wait a sec," Maudie said now, as we hesitated near

Ms. Dwyer's door. She bent down to the little drinking fountain and pressed the button. Water suddenly splashed up at her face. "What a slob I am!" she said, jumping back.

"You're not," I said. "You're just nervous, that's all. Me too." My throat was dry. I bent down and took a long drink.

We stood by the fountain a minute, wiping off our faces and adjusting our books. Then we grinned at each other, pulled the door open, and went in.

The kids looked up, and then they all started yelling at once. "They're here!" "Hi, Kate! Hi, Maudie!" "Ms. Dwyer, here they are!" A little boy pulled at my sleeve. "We went to the nurse's office!" Simon came and stood beside me, smiling shyly.

"It's good to see you!" Ms. Dwyer said from across the room. "You've brought books. Shall we start right in with them? People! Let's make our reading circle."

The kids began to shove chairs around, calling "Sit here!" and "Sit next to me!" and tugging at us. There seemed to be more of them than I had remembered. I couldn't think of anyone's name, except Simon.

Ms. Dwyer set a chair between two little boys. "Maudie and Kate will sit here to read," she said firmly.

Slowly, the rest of the circle took shape. The kids wiggled in their seats, poking each other.

"Let's settle down now," Ms. Dwyer said. "Maudie, would you like to read first?"

Maudie glanced nervously at me and went to sit in

the empty chair. I found myself a seat outside the circle. The kids stared expectantly at Maudie.

She tucked her skirt carefully around her legs, shifted in the chair, and held up her book. "This book is called *Little Bear*," she said. Her voice came out nervously.

The kids started to yell. "We *have* that book!" "We already know it!"

Maudie looked helplessly over at Ms. Dwyer.

"It's *always* nice to hear *Little Bear* again," Ms. Dwyer said quickly, reaching over to a tiny girl with pigtails who was poking the girl next to her. "And we're going to give Maudie our best attention, aren't we, Alexandra?"

Alexandra nodded solemnly and Maudie began again. " 'It is cold, ' " she read.

"I can't *see!*" interrupted a boy with a curly Afro. "Ms. Dwyer, Jimmy's in my *way!*"

"Just push your chair over a little bit, Richard," Ms. Dwyer said calmly. "Myra, move yours so Richard has room."

Maudie cleared her throat. " 'It is cold. See the snow—' "

"*We* have snow!" A blond-haired girl pointed out the window.

"Be *quiet!*" somebody yelled. "I can't hear!"

They weren't even letting her start! But Maudie leaned forward as though she was going to tell an important secret, and began again. "It's snowy in the story, just like in Sussex," she said in a firmer tone.

"And Little Bear doesn't have a jacket like ours. Let's see how he keeps himself warm."

"I know!" yelled Myra. "He—"

But Maudie was reading on in a determined voice. By the time she had turned a few pages, everyone was listening. Maudie went on quietly, stopping to ask questions about the pictures. The kids answered in their ordinary voices. She was doing it!

By the time she got to the last line—"Good night, Little Bear. Sleep well"—I was so caught up in the story that I almost forgot where I was.

Maudie closed the book. "The end," she said.

Everyone clapped.

Maudie stood up and came over to me, looking pleased.

"You were good!" I said.

"Thank you, Maudie," said Ms. Dwyer. "You can see we all enjoyed the story. Are you ready now, Kate?"

This was it. I walked to the chair with everyone's eyes on me and sat down. Maudie was smiling encouragingly. I held up my book.

"This is a story about a boy who wants a dog for his birthday," I said. "It's called *The Birthday Dog.*"

The room exploded.

"*My* birthday's next week!"

"Mine's in August!"

"I have a dog named Penny!"

Simon didn't say anything, but he was smiling.

I started in. " 'For his sixth birthday, Benjamin

wanted a dog more than anything else in the world.' "

"My *friend*'s name is Benjamin!" Alexandra jumped up triumphantly. "He—"

"That's nice," I said quickly, hurrying on before she could describe her friend. At this rate, I'd be sitting there on page one when the end-of-school bell rang. In the corner of my eye I saw Ms. Dwyer nodding encouragingly. I raised my voice. " 'When Benjamin woke up, the first thing he thought was, "It's my birthday!" The second thing was, "I'm getting a puppy." The third thing was, "I hope." ' "

Suddenly, I could feel their attention. I turned the page and pointed to the picture. " 'Benjamin looked quickly around the room. There was no dog.' "

A little sigh went around the circle. I read on quickly to get to the good part. When Benjamin opened the birthday card that said he was going to get one of Blackie's puppies, there was a gasp of pleasure. And two pages on, when Benjamin and his father hurried next door to see the puppies get born, the children leaned forward breathlessly. The room was hushed as I read the words. " 'Just then, Blackie gave a little moan, and her stomach began to ripple.' "

"It's starting to be born!" someone whispered.

" 'A small, wet shape began to come out of Blackie,' " I read. " 'She pushed hard again, until all of it was out.' "

"It doesn't look like a puppy," Myra said softly.

"That's just what Benjamin thought," I told her. " 'But then,' " I read on quickly, " 'Blackie began to

47

bite gently at the thin sac that covered the puppy like a blanket. She licked it all over with her tongue, until it was clean.'" I turned the page. "And there it is!" I said, pointing to the picture of the little newborn puppy.

"I see it!" they shouted.

"It's so *little!*"

"It's so *cute!*"

"*My* puppy is cute," Simon said softly.

All of a sudden I wasn't nervous at all. I was actually enjoying myself! I'd been so worried about holding their attention and keeping them quiet, but now I saw that wasn't the point. Reading out loud to young children was more like talking back and forth. I shifted on the little chair and went on with the story, stopping for their comments. There was a kind of rhythm to it. When I came to the last sentence, "'And Benjamin was sure that Happy was the best birthday present in the whole world,'" there was a general sigh of content. And then they all clapped for *me*.

"Thank you, Kate," said Ms. Dwyer. "That was *such* a nice book." She looked around the circle. "Does anyone want to ask Kate about it, or tell something about puppies?" I think she was hoping Simon would speak up.

And he did. "How did the puppy get in there?" he asked quietly.

I wasn't sure what he meant. "Get where, Simon?"

"In *there*. Inside his mommy."

I hadn't expected that! I looked at Ms. Dwyer. She

was nodding as though I should go ahead and explain, but I didn't know how to. Frantically, I tried to think of a good way to say it.

"Well," I began, "before the puppy starts at all the father dog—" I hesitated. I didn't want to get embarrassed. That would be so childish.

"He plants a seed in the mommy!" someone finished for me.

What had I gotten into? "That's right," I said, trying to sound matter-of-fact. "Before the puppy begins, the father dog and the mother dog mate." I tried to remember how Mom had explained it when I was their age. "And this little tiny thing called a sperm goes into the mother—"

"Into her *vagina!*" Alexandra shouted.

I looked at Ms. Dwyer. She leaned forward in her chair as though she was ready to take over if I needed help.

"That's right, Alexandra," I said weakly. "And then—"

"*I* have a vagina!" Myra yelled.

"Me, too!" some of the other girls shouted. A few of them looked at me sort of blankly.

I didn't know what to say.

"I have a penis!" Richard said loudly. "Boys have penises!"

Some of the boys began to jump around. "I do, too!" "Me, too!"

Oh, man—they were never going to stop!

Then Ms. Dwyer broke in calmly. "That's right,"

* 49

she said. "Now, let's all sit down and see if we can talk quietly." A couple of kids were giggling, but most of them listened intently as Ms. Dwyer got back to puppies. "As Kate said, after the father dog and the mother dog mate, a tiny little puppy begins to grow inside the mother dog."

There was a thoughtful hush as they took that in. I was really hoping there wouldn't be any more questions. What if they brought up *human* mothers and fathers? Little kids can come out with anything. I didn't know what I'd say if they asked about that.

"You know what?" Jimmy shouted into the silence.

"What?" I asked desperately. What *next*?

"My dog's name is Prince!" Jimmy said triumphantly.

I was so relieved I almost laughed. "That's a wonderful name," I said gratefully.

Then they all began to tell me their dogs' names and their cats' names, and guinea pig names and even turtle names. I started to feel in control again. I called on different kids, realizing with surprise that I knew a lot of their names. I felt almost like a teacher. It was neat.

Then Ms. Dwyer looked at the clock. "It's nearly time for the bell!" she said in surprise. "Where did the time go?" She smiled at the children. "What shall we say to Maudie and Kate?"

"Thank you!" they yelled at us.

Ms. Dwyer told them to get their coats, and then she came over to us. "You were marvelous," she said, "both of you." She turned to me. "You handled their comments nicely, Kate. Kids this age can be embarrassingly frank! But I don't want them to think there's anything wrong with their natural curiosity. I'm glad you could answer them so matter-of-factly."

"I *was* sort of embarrassed," I confessed. "I never expected them to bring up all that stuff."

"They're eager to talk about everything," Ms. Dwyer said. "That's why I like teaching first graders so much." She reached out to help Myra with her jacket. "Wasn't this a nice reading time, Myra?"

Myra nodded seriously. "When are you coming back?" she asked us.

"Soon," Maudie promised.

"I'll be in touch," Ms. Dwyer said. "You and Grace Plotkin and I should get together to plan your next visits. I'd really like you to work with the children individually. They'd love that."

Simon came over to me. His mittens dangled from his jacket sleeves on a string.

"So long, Simon," I said, touching his blond head. I almost said "So long, honey," I felt so loving toward him. Toward all of them. It's amazing how sweet little children are.

Everyone yelled good-bye as Maudie and I went out of the door. We waved back. Then we turned and collapsed onto each other, laughing.

"You were terrific!" Maudie said. "I would have died if I'd been you when they started asking those embarrassing questions!" She giggled. "And yelling all those *things*."

"I *know* it. *I* nearly died." I put my arm across Maudie's shoulders and we headed for the door. "You were really good, too," I told her. "They loved your book." Our steps echoed pleasantly in the empty hall. "Hey, Maudie," I said. "We *did* it!"

Neither of us had the slightest idea that we'd done anything *wrong*.

chapter 8

* * *

AND NOTHING that happened that weekend gave me any warning.

The telephone was ringing as I walked into the kitchen Saturday morning. I started for it, but Josh got there first. He acts as though he owns the phone sometimes. He's always calling Denise or expecting a call from her. He should realize that I have friends who might be trying to get *me*.

Anyway, this call wasn't for either of us.

"Just a minute," Josh said, rolling his eyes at me. "Dad!" he yelled upstairs. "It's Mr. Miller."

"Coming," Dad yelled down in an irritated voice. Josh put one hand over the mouthpiece and waved the other at me, mimicking Mr. Miller. "Blah, blah, blah," he mouthed.

I snickered.

"Got it, Josh," Dad called.

Josh hung up the receiver. "Morning, Bigfoot."

"Josh!" He has some nerve.

I got myself a banana and poured some cereal into a bowl. I used to like to make bacon and eggs on Saturdays, but there's not that much pleasure in it anymore, with Josh making retching noises at the bacon smell.

"Want to visit Aunt Lucy with me later?" I asked.

"I can't," he said right away. "I'm going down to the harbor." That's where Denise lives.

"Boy, you must really be in love," I said. "It seems like you're always hanging out at Denise's." In a way, I felt sort of hurt. Josh and I used to do stuff together on Saturdays. It's Mom and Dad's busiest day. People who can't get off during the week want to look at houses on the weekends. I feel sorry for my parents sometimes, the same way I do for bus drivers or hotdog sellers who work on holidays.

"It just so happens I'm going there to *study*," Josh said in a dignified tone. "I have a geometry exam Monday, and Denise's notes are better than mine."

"Yeah, well, keep your mind on your books."

"Hey, kiddo—don't get fresh!" Josh hunched himself into his gorilla pose and lurched toward me. "*Aaaaaaarh!*" he yelled, thumping his chest. He grabbed me around the neck.

"*Josh!*" I pulled him off.

"Really, Josh," Mom said, coming into the kitchen with Dad. "I thought you'd grown out of that!"

"He just grew into a bigger gorilla," I said, laughing

in spite of myself as Josh scratched himself thoughtfully under the armpit. He does a really good ape act. When I was little, he could actually scare me with it.

"What did the Millers want this time?" Josh asked.

"A plumber!" Mom said, in an annoyed tone. "At least, that's what they *need*. What they *want* is for your father to drop all his appointments on the busiest day of the week and rush over there to fix a leaky toilet."

"I'll never understand," Dad said, spooning out instant coffee, "why some clients expect the agent who sells them a house to be responsible for everything that goes wrong with it for the next twenty years." He gave Mom a mug of coffee, and they sat down at the table.

"It makes you grateful for people like the Liebermans," Mom said to him. She turned to Josh and me. "We're taking them back to the Shore Road house today. They've just about decided to buy it. I hope they do. They seem like awfully nice people. Very easygoing and pleasant."

"Wait till their toilet springs a leak," Dad said, joking. "No, you're right, Nina. I liked them from the first." He stood up. "I'd better start the car."

"Will you make a lot on the sale?" I asked Mom. She and Dad aren't like some parents—they discuss money and business affairs with us. The real estate business hadn't been that good lately, because of inflation. Houses were unusually expensive. When Mom and Dad sold a house they got a bigger commission, but buyers were so cautious that it took them a long time to make any sale.

"It'll come to a sizable fee," Mom said. "*If* they

*55

decide to take it." She set down her mug. "Did you kids remember about Aunt Lucy?"

"*I'm* going." I looked meaningfully at Josh. "Josh has to *study*."

"At the library?" Mom asked innocently.

Josh almost blushed. "At Denise's," he said. "We're studying together."

"Oh, Josh," Mom said quickly. "I hate having you bother the McConnells all the time. Don't you think you could study by yourself for once?"

I think Mom's worried about Josh having a girl friend. I've overheard her discussing "teen-age romances" on the phone in an anxious way. It's funny— with me, I sometimes wonder if she thinks I *should* have a boy friend. The thing is, mothers can worry in any direction.

"It's better to study with another person," I said, to get Josh off the hook. But I couldn't resist a nudge. "Especially if that person took better notes than you, *and* has long blond hair."

"Come on, Katie," Josh said quickly. "I'll ride down to Shore Road with you." He went for his jacket, and I packed up some things for Aunt Lucy—cookies, an orange, and the puppy book, which I was planning to read her.

Aunt Lucy reads everything—Shakespeare, the Bible, murder mysteries. She likes me to read aloud to her too. I thought she'd enjoy *The Birthday Dog* because she's had lots of dogs in her life.

We decided to go the back way, down Woods Road. It's longer but prettier. You go past the oldest house in

Sussex, a little frame cottage that's a doctor's office now, but that a cousin of my mother's used to own when Josh and I were little, so we played there sometimes. There are lots of old houses around it. Most of them have numbers on them, like 1710, or even 1600 something, to tell the year they were built.

The wind was against us so Josh and I didn't talk much. Still, it was nice just riding along together. At the corner of Shore Road Josh turned off for Denise's.

"Tell Aunt Lucy I'll come next week," he called.

"O.K. Tell Denise not to forget the geometry!"

I pedaled hard to get up speed, and coasted down the last two blocks to the nursing home. An old man in a knit ski cap with a pompon sat on a bench by the door.

"Come to see Aunt Lucy, have you?" he asked.

"Yep." Everyone at the nursing home calls Aunt Lucy "Aunt," even though some of them are almost as old as she is.

"You'll find her in the lounge," the man said. "Playing Scrabble, as usual. Taking on all challengers, beating every one."

Aunt Lucy's a famous Scrabble player. She's unusually good. I hardly ever win when I play her.

But when I went into the lounge, the Scrabble board was put away and Aunt Lucy was staring out the window, looking glum. A few other people, two of them in wheelchairs, sat in the room. I went over and kissed Aunt Lucy. She has a whiskery cheek. "Hi, Aunt Lucy," I said loudly. She's quite deaf, so you have to yell at her.

She looked up, startled. Then she smiled. "Well, hello, sweetie." She patted my cheek. "It's lovely to see you. My, your cheeks are cold—did you walk over?"

"Biked," I shouted. "How're you feeling today?" I feel sort of stupid yelling when other people are around. Still, I think some of them like listening in. That way they sort of share the visit. A tiny woman on the couch across from us was smiling at me now, and a couple of other people stared at us with pleased interest.

Aunt Lucy pulled me down to her. "Mrs. White cheated," she said loudly into my ear, nodding toward the woman in a wheelchair by the door. "That's why she won. Pretended to drop some letters on the floor, reached right down and picked up the E she needed."

"She probably didn't mean to drop them," I shouted, embarrassed. Aunt Lucy has a pretty sharp tongue. Sometimes I think she *wants* people to over-hear her. Out of the corner of my eye I saw Mrs. White turn her chair around and wheel herself out the door. I hoped her feelings weren't hurt.

"She was losing," Aunt Lucy insisted sharply. "Without that E she would have lost for sure." Then she noticed my bag. "What have you brought with you?" she asked.

"Chocolate chip cookies and an orange." I gave her the bag.

"Chocolate chip has always been my favorite," Aunt Lucy said, pleased as a little child. In a funny way, she sometimes reminds me of a child. The nurses braid her white hair each morning, and fasten the braids with rubber bands, like a little girl's. Her legs are thin and her stomach is round, and her feet don't reach the floor when she sits in one of the big lounge chairs. Even her wrinkles and whiskers make you think of a little child who's been made up to act Grandma in a kindergarten play of Red Riding Hood.

Aunt Lucy was chewing her cookie with relish. "Is that a book you've brought me?"

"I wanted to show it to you," I yelled. "It's about a puppy—it's a book I read at Concord School yesterday."

Around the lounge, people leaned forward. The bent old man in the wheelchair nudged himself toward us with trembling hands, blinking and smiling.

Aunt Lucy held the book up to her eyes. "Oh, isn't he the dearest little thing!" she said, peering at the cover photo of Happy in Benjamin's arms. "You say you read this at *Concord?*" She looked perplexed. "I thought you were up at Revere School this year." For her age, she's got a fantastic memory.

"I am! I just went to Concord to read to the children," I explained.

"Isn't that nice! Like a teacher!" Aunt Lucy looked proudly around the room, obviously wanting the others to hear this. "A teacher," she repeated loudly. "Well. And you're going to read the book to me?"

"Yep." I pulled my chair close and held the book up so she could make out the pictures. " 'For his sixth birthday, Benjamin wanted a dog more than anything else in the world,' " I read.

By now I had practically memorized the words. Since I didn't have to watch each page closely, I could see what was happening in the lounge. The man in the wheelchair had pushed himself toward us and everyone else had stopped talking to listen.

Just then a nurse came into the lounge. She looked around, took in what was happening, and came over. "Excuse me, Aunt Lucy," she said loudly. "I hate to interrupt, but I believe *all* these folks here would like to share the story with you. If I just arrange some chairs—"

Aunt Lucy looked cross for a second. Then she smiled grandly. "Oh, well. Let them listen. Since none of *them* has a visitor to read to them." Aunt Lucy's very vain about the attention she gets, and the number of visitors she has. She loves being the oldest person in the home.

The nurse smiled at me. "I'll just go out and find Mrs. White—she'd hate to miss out on this."

"What'd she say?" Aunt Lucy demanded.

"She's going to get Mrs. White."

Aunt Lucy made a wry face. "Oh, well, might as well let the poor thing come along," she said complacently. "It'll take her mind off her complaints."

I looked around as the people in the lounge settled themselves, waiting for the nurse to come back. I knew most of them by now. When I first went to the nursing home it had been strange to see so many old people in one place. It was hard not to stare at some of them as they inched along the halls in walkers and wheelchairs. I used to try to visit Aunt Lucy alone, but she liked to take me around and introduce me to her friends, and after I got to know more of the old people I stopped feeling uncomfortable with them. They always acted so glad to see me. The people in the lounge were smiling at me now as they waited patiently for the reading to go on.

Then the nurse came in, pushing Mrs. White toward us.

"We won't start all over for you, Clara," Aunt Lucy announced firmly. "You'll just have to pick up from where we are." She bent toward me and whispered loudly, "That'll serve her right for cheating!"

Quickly, I held up the book and went on with Benjamin's story, saying the words very clearly and slowly so they would all understand. There were pleased little murmurs when Benjamin read his birthday card, and everyone was as excited as the first-grade children had been when the puppy was born. I turned the pages slowly, saying the words by heart. When I had finished the last page, the old people still leaned forward expectantly. "The end," I said, to let them know it was over.

They clapped, just like the little kids.

Aunt Lucy patted my arm. "Thank you, Kate. That brought back happy memories of all the puppies I've seen born."

"A wonderful book—a wonderful reader!" said the trembly old man, blinking and shaking in his chair.

"There are so many good books for children these days!" the nurse said. "Wasn't it sweet of Kate to share this one with us?"

I rode back home feeling quite proud of myself. I couldn't wait to call Maudie up and tell her what a success the book had been at the nursing home. Maybe she'd come with me sometime and show them *Little Bear*. And we could take other books, too, as the project went on. It would be neat to tell Ms. Plotkin about reading at the nursing home on Monday.

Boy. Was I in for a surprise.

chapter 9
*** * **

"KATE, may I see you for just a minute?" Ms. Plotkin drew me over as soon as I walked into class on Monday. She had a funny look on her face. "I need to talk with you and Maudie."

"Sure." I followed her toward her desk. What was this about?

She hesitated, watching the door. "Morning, Billy. Hi, Laura, Jackie." Jackie gave me a quizzical look. "Hello, Steve." Ms. Plotkin raised her voice as the rest of the kids piled in. "Good morning, all of you. Will you settle down quickly and start reading Chapter Four in your workbooks for a few minutes? I have some business to attend to right now. Oh, hi, Maudie," she said, as Maudie hurried in. "Will you come over here a second before you sit down?"

Maudie came over eagerly. She had on a blue velour shirt that I hadn't seen before. It was neat.

"What a pretty top, Maudie," Ms. Plotkin said pleasantly. She put an arm around each of us and pulled us close.

"Girls," she said soberly, "I don't know how to begin telling you this, so I'll just jump right in. Mr. Staley wants to see the three of us in his office five minutes from now." She broke off and turned to face the room, which had suddenly quieted. Everyone was staring at us. "Hey, kids!" she said to them. "I'd like to have a private conversation up here, if you don't mind. Will you get out your books, as I asked, and start reading?"

"Which books?" people started asking. "What chapter are we supposed to read?" Billy Taylor stood up and headed for the pencil sharpener.

Maudie and I looked at each other. What was happening?

"Sit *down*, Billy," Ms. Plotkin said sharply. "Everyone—cut out the racket. It's not too much to ask of you, is it, to open your workbooks to Chapter Four and begin reading? Right *now*. I don't want to hear any unnecessary noise."

I'd never heard her speak in such an irritated way. She's usually so easy. "Here's the thing," she said more quietly, turning back to us. "It seems that over the weekend there've been some complaints about one of the books you read to Anne Dwyer's kids." She looked at me, squeezing my shoulder. "The puppy book," she said.

I jumped.

"Mr. Hofsteder got two calls from disturbed parents on Saturday and three or four more yesterday," Ms. Plotkin went on. "Last night he talked with Anne and me at Anne's place, and then we all went over to Mr. Staley's home and met with him. Mr. Staley feels—"

"What *kind* of complaints?" I broke in. "What's the matter with the book? The kids loved it!"

Maudie looked stunned. "Ms. Dwyer did, too," she said vehemently. And *you* said—"

"I know," Ms. Plotkin said quickly. "I said it was a good choice. It was. The first thing I want you both to know is that I take full responsibility for whatever problem exists. Anne feels responsible, too, but I think I'm most to blame—" She turned suddenly. "Jackie Schaefer, will you *please*, for five minutes, stop that incessant note-passing! Just give the note back to her, Billy. She can tell Laura whatever she has to say when this class is over. Now, hit those books—I mean all of you—and don't let me hear another word." She sighed.

"Kate," she said gently. "What seems to have bothered some of the first-grade parents is, first of all, the illustration of the mother dog giving birth, and then the discussion you had about mating. Now I know it's a perfectly straightforward picture," she went on quickly before I could protest, "and Anne says she was very impressed with the way you managed the discussion."

"She was terrific, Ms. Plotkin," Maudie put in passionately. "I would have been all embarrassed if it was me, but Kate acted so natural, and the kids were really interested, you could tell." Her voice rose. Around the room, kids looked up. "It isn't *fair* for those parents to complain. How do *they* know what happened? They weren't even there!" Maudie went on.

"That's right," Ms. Plotkin said. "Not only that, but they haven't read the book either." She almost smiled. "Or hadn't, anyway, most of them, until one mother rushed to the library and took out their only other copy, which has probably circulated all over town by this morning." She looked at the clock. "Oh, dear, we're late for Mr. Staley already. I wish he hadn't insisted on seeing us the first thing. I feel terrible just throwing all this at you, having to drag you down there—"

"It's O.K., Ms. Plotkin," I said, suddenly realizing what a bad situation this could be for her. She'd said she was responsible—what if Mr. Staley made her take the whole blame? "It's not your fault," I said comfortingly. "I was the one who picked out the book."

"It isn't anyone's fault," Maudie said angrily. "What *fault* is there in reading a good book? I mean, if it was a horrible book or something, why would the library even *have* it?"

"Yeah," I agreed. "Gerda Whitman—she's related to me—helped me find it! Those parents should talk to *her!*"

"They have," said Ms. Plotkin wearily. "Anne thought to get in touch with Gerda last night. She told us people had been streaming into the children's room all day, asking for the book. Gerda's caught up in all this too, I'm afraid. A lot of people will be, if we don't get it settled quickly. Now, come on—we must go." She faced the class. "Kids, Kate and Maudie and I are going down to see Mr. Staley for a short while. Give me a break and act like responsible human beings while I'm out of the room, can you?"

Hands shot up everywhere. "Ms. Plotkin—"

"I don't have time for questions," she said quickly. "I'm just trusting you to behave yourselves. If you finish Chapter Four, go right on to Chapter Five."

Maudie and I followed her out the door. I looked back for a second. Jackie was bent over Christine's desk, whispering furiously. Everybody was whispering and staring at us. It made me feel awful.

Ms. Plotkin hurried us down the hall. "I don't want you to get upset," she said as we rushed along, "no matter what Mr. Staley asks you. Remember, he's responsible for everything that goes on in this school, including our project. He's been taking a lot of flak from parents all weekend. He may sound upset, but I'm convinced that he'll be supportive." She didn't sound that convinced.

Maudie grabbed my arm. "It'll turn out O.K. Don't worry."

I nodded, but I was worried. I was scared!

Ms. Plotkin practically ran down the stairs. At the office door she stopped and tugged her shirt straight. "O.K., kids?"

"O.K.," we said.

Ms. Plotkin opened the door and we went in.

*67

The secretary pointed to the inner office. "Go right on in. Mr. Staley's waiting for you."

Mr. Staley sat behind his desk, frowning at some papers. His office was full of filing cabinets and bookshelves. A rolled-up movie screen leaned against one wall, next to a framed plaque of some poem. The poem started with the word IF in big letters.

"Sit down," Mr. Staley said, looking up as though we'd interrupted him.

There were only two chairs. Ms. Plotkin sat down on the one by the desk. Maudie went into the outer office and brought back another chair. When she set it down, she bumped against the movie screen, which crashed to the floor. "Excuse me," Maudie mumbled, blushing.

I helped her stand it back up. Then we both sat down and waited for Mr. Staley to begin.

He stared at us over his glasses. "Now, let's get the facts straight, Miss Plotkin," he said. "I want to check every detail with these girls."

Maudie shifted nervously beside me.

"Which of you read the book in question aloud?" Mr. Staley asked.

"I did." I cleared my throat. "I—"

"Do you have it here?" Mr. Staley demanded.

"No. It's at home. I never thought of bringing it. I didn't know anyone would want to see it."

"A great many people want to see that book," Mr. Staley said. "Including myself." He pushed his glasses up. "But a Mrs. Bergen, who apparently secured another copy from the library, will be bringing it with her when she comes to see me this afternoon."

"Good," said Ms. Plotkin quickly. "I'm eager for you to read the book, Mr. Staley. So you can see for yourself how innocuous it is."

I didn't know what that word meant, but I was glad Ms. Plotkin had spoken so firmly. She didn't sound scared of Mr. Staley.

"For the moment," Mr. Staley said, "let's concentrate on the discussion that apparently took place after the reading." He leaned toward me, rolling a pencil in his fingers. "Now, young lady—" He turned to Ms. Plotkin. "Which one of them is the Harris girl?"

"I am." I could talk for myself! "This is Maudie Schmidt."

"Yes." Mr. Staley looked us over as though he was checking whether I'd got it right. "Your brother's one of our better students," he said to me.

"*Kate*'s a fine student," said Ms. Plotkin quickly. "And so is Maudie. That's one reason I was so pleased to have them initiate our project."

"All right, Kate," said Mr. Staley. "Please describe the discussion that followed your reading of the book. Try to remember exactly what was said."

"Well," I began nervously. This was so embarrassing! How was I going to talk about mating with Mr. Staley? Or mention a word like *penis?* "Well, first of all," I said, to get it straight, "the discussion went on all through the book, not just afterward. The kids kept interrupting to say things."

"Can you give me an example?" asked Mr. Staley.

"Well, like saying they had a dog and stuff," I said cautiously.

"They were all excited when the puppies got born," Maudie put in.

"All right." Mr. Staley cut her off. "Go on, Kate."

"Well, when I finished the book, one boy asked me how the puppies got there. He meant, how they got started inside the mother." Absent-mindedly, I started reading the poem on the wall above Mr. Staley's head. "IF you can keep your head when all about you are losing theirs . . ." it began.

That was a big if. I forced myself to look Mr. Staley in the eye. "So I said that first the father dog and the mother dog had to mate—"

"Is that the precise word you used?" Mr. Staley interrupted.

I nodded. "I said the father dog puts the sperm into the mother—" I took a breath. Beside me, Maudie coughed nervously. Ms. Plotkin leaned forward. "And then a girl said, 'In her vagina." I rushed on, trying to keep my voice steady. "And then some children said *they* had vaginas. Or penises—"

Mr. Staley cleared his throat. I suddenly had this embarrassing thought that *he* had a penis. I nearly died.

"I guess that's about all," I finished lamely.

Mr. Staley leaned back against his chair. He looked over at Ms. Plotkin and almost smiled, in a grim kind of way. "I'm afraid it's enough," he said, looking stern again. "More than enough, for some of our parents.

When you've been in this school district as long as I have, Miss Plotkin, you'll appreciate some of the public relations problems we face. Fully half my time on this job is spent with parents. He sighed. "A situation like this doesn't make it any easier."

"Oh, I'm sure," Ms. Plotkin said sympathetically. "If I'd had any idea—"

"That's the trouble," Mr. Staley said. "People need to *anticipate*. Younger teachers like you and Miss Dwyer often underestimate the anxiety parents feel. They depend on us to select materials wisely, to teach conscientiously—"

"Oh, I *do!*" said Ms. Plotkin earnestly. "I'm terribly sorry if any parent was offended by what went on at Concord, but I have to say that I can't find anything wrong with either the book Kate chose or the discussion it led to."

To my surprise, Mr. Staley said, "The book sounds innocent enough." He actually smiled. "Though I must admit I wish it hadn't been quite so anatomical." He paused. "But I'm afraid the parents who are bothered by it can make a good deal of trouble for us." He pushed his chair back and stood up. "I think I have all the information I need. I'll let you know the results of my parent conference this afternoon. Naturally," he added, "we'll have to discontinue the interschool project for the time being."

Maudie and I looked at each other and then at Ms. Plotkin.

"I understand," she said quietly. "All right, girls—" She stood up. "Thank you, Mr. Staley," she said,

*71

reaching across the desk to shake his hand. "I appreciate your support."

I wondered if we were supposed to shake hands too, but Mr. Staley just nodded in our direction. "Goodbye, girls," he said. "I'll expect you to keep our discussion confidential."

Maudie and I mumbled that we would. Then we all went out.

"Boy!" I said, as soon as the office door had closed behind us. "What's going to happen now, Ms. Plotkin? Do you think they might stop the project for good?"

She patted my arm. "I don't know, Kate. We'll just have to wait and see."

chapter 10

* * *

BY LUNCH TIME, it was all over school. It's amazing how people can latch on to a few simple facts and blow them into gigantic rumors. I don't know how all the stories got started. Of course, everyone in Ms. Plotkin's class had seen us go down to the office, but that didn't explain it. Ms. Plotkin hadn't said anything when we got back, even though you could tell all the kids were curious. Ms. Plotkin just started right in on a discussion of the subjunctive clause that lasted until the bell. Jackie had passed me a note—"What *happened?*" it said—but I just shrugged, and after class Maudie and I ducked out before anyone could intercept us.

"Take care," Ms. Plotkin called after us. "I'll be in touch."

Maudie and I talked in low voices as we went down

the hall, so no one could have overheard us—and if they had, they wouldn't have found out much. We were too stunned by everything to make any sense. We kept going over what Mr. Staley had said, getting madder and madder.

"I can't believe it!" Maudie whispered fiercely, yanking at the strap of her book bag. "Can you imagine people calling Mr. Hofsteder up without even waiting to get the facts from Ms. Dwyer?"

"I know it. And rushing over to the library—Gerda must have thought they were nuts!"

"They *are* nuts," Maudie said. "Acting like it's a dirty book or something, for Pete's sake."

"And like *I'm* dirty," I said furiously. "As though *I* brought up all that stuff about, you know." I looked around and lowered my voice even more. "*Penises* and stuff. What'd they want me to do, make up sappy little names instead of using real words? *That's* dirty, if you ask me."

"Yeah," Maudie agreed. "Like when they call it 'down below' or something. That really embarrasses me."

"Me, too!" It was surprising how alike Maudie and I were in some ways.

We came to the door of her math room and Maudie leaned against it, letting her book bag slip to the floor. "Listen, Kate," she said solemnly. "Whatever happens, I'm standing by you."

"Thanks!" I watched her go in, feeling very grateful that she'd been through everything with me. It would

have been awful to be the only kid who was involved. Not that Maudie was actually involved—nobody had complained about *her* book. That made it even nicer of her to be so loyal.

Kids kept coming up to me all morning, trying to find out what was happening. A couple of people wanted to know the name of the book I'd read, and one girl I didn't even know, from another grade, stopped me on my way into the cafeteria to ask if it was true that I'd told some little kids all about sex.

"No, about *dogs*." I turned away angrily and almost collided with Josh. "Josh!" I said in surprise. "What are *you* doing here?"

He pulled me over to the cafeteria wall. "What's going on, Katie? Are you O.K.? A kid in geometry said his parents heard my sister was in trouble for reading a dirty book at Concord. I told him it couldn't be you, but then someone else came up with this bogus story about sex education, and another kid told me you'd been down at Mr. Staley's office." He put his hand on the wall above my shoulder and leaned down. "What's up, anyway?"

"Oh, Josh, it's horrible!" For the first time that day, I felt like crying. "I didn't do *anything!* It's just that a lot of parents complained about my book, the one I read at Concord. They called up Mr. Hofsteder and Mr. Staley, and they're even after Gerda for having the book in the library." Telling him was a relief. "So now it's all over the whole school, and everybody's acting like I'm some kind of a monster, and the

project's been stopped—" I hadn't really taken that in up to now. "All the kids were just starting to *like* me!" I said bitterly.

"Wait a sec," Josh said. "Just because a few parents complained doesn't mean anything. They probably haven't even *read* the book. When they do, they'll see that there's nothing wrong with it."

"Well, *some* people think there is. They think there's something wrong with *me!*" I looked around the cafeteria for Maudie. "Kids are staring at us right now!" I said. "I feel like a pariah!" Pariahs were an outcast group in India that everyone avoided. We learned about them last year at Emerson.

"Don't let them get to you," Josh said. "Listen, I have to get back. Keep cool—don't tell people anything. It's none of their business." He smiled grimly. "Wait till Mom and Dad hear about this—they'll make a bigger fuss than the other parents. Man, they're going to be furious!" He bopped my shoulder. "Hang in there, kiddo."

It was good he brought up Mom and Dad—I hadn't thought about them. They *would* be furious when they heard people were complaining about my book, and they'd say so. My parents always fight back if they think someone's being unfair to their kids.

"Thanks, Josh," I said as he turned to go. "It was nice of you to come down here, no kidding."

Josh waved and went out.

Kids were thumping trays down on tables, yelling, pulling benches around. It was horribly noisy, as usual. Maudie wasn't at any of the back tables. I saw

Jackie and Christine at ours. I didn't feel up to eating with them. I didn't feel that much like eating, actually. The steamy meat smell from the lunch counter was sickening. I wonder how Josh stands it. I pressed my back against the wall, trying to decide where to go. I could just feel everyone staring at me. Sometimes I wish there was a private kids' dining room, like the teachers', where you could go to eat lunch in peace. Everything is so *public* in school.

"Hey, Kate!" Rosemary rushed up, looking worried. "What's going *on?* Everybody's saying these crazy things—"

"It's nothing," I said shortly. "Never mind. If people want to get all worked up about something without even knowing the facts, *let* them."

Rosemary touched my arm. "I know it's none of my business," she said. "Except—if someone's making you upset for no reason, I just wanted to tell you not to feel bad."

She looked so concerned that I was sorry I'd jumped at her. It wasn't *her* fault, after all. "Oh, Rosie," I burst out, "it's so awful. Everyone's mad because of a book I read at Concord—" I stopped. "Listen, don't say anything, O.K.? I'm not supposed to talk about it."

"Sure," Rosemary said seriously. "I wouldn't."

"It wasn't a dumb book or anything, Rosemary," I went on. "It wasn't dirty, either, honestly. It was just this story about a boy who sees his birthday puppy get born. It's a good book. Ms. Plotkin even said so."

"So why's everyone complaining?"

"*I* don't know." I hesitated. "Well, I do, really. See,

it wasn't just the book. It was partly that, and partly what the kids said after I read it." To my surprise, I giggled. "You should have heard them, Rosie. All these little boys were jumping around and yelling about their *penises!*"

"You're kidding!" Rosemary giggled too. "Oh, *Kate!*"

"It's not funny," I said, laughing in spite of myself. "It's horrible!" Once I'd started laughing I couldn't seem to stop. "And the girls were shouting about their *vaginas!*" I croaked out, leaning against Rosemary. I couldn't believe that the whole situation hadn't struck me funny before. It was hysterical! I shuddered with laughter, feeling the hiccups coming on.

"What's wrong, Kate?" I hadn't seen Maudie come in, I was laughing so hard.

"Nothing!" I choked, my stomach aching from the hiccup. "I just started telling Rosemary the whole story, and it suddenly struck me funny!"

Maudie grinned. "You know what was really funny? Mr. Staley's face this morning, when you talked about, you know—"

"*Did* you?" Now Rosemary was laughing. "With Mr. *Staley!* Oh, Kate, did you actually mention—"

I practically exploded. "Yeah, and I thought I'd die!" By now all three of us were howling. All of a sudden I felt a lot better. "Hey, we should eat," I said. "Lunch period's going to be over."

There was no line, so we walked right through. I paid first and was standing there waiting for Rosemary and Maudie when it hit me. Where were we going to sit? I'd never eaten with Maudie before. I looked over at our table. Jackie and Christine were still there. If I took her over, would they mind?

Maudie was hesitating by the cashier's stool, looking embarrassed.

"Come on," Rosemary said briskly. "We'll be late."

At first I thought she was being insensitive, but then she added, "Hurry up, Maudie," in the most natural complaining way, and I realized it was the opposite. She was inviting Maudie to sit at our table without making a big thing of it. I followed the two of them down the aisle, hoping Jackie wouldn't say anything rude. If she did—

But Jackie hardly glanced at Maudie as she climbed awkwardly over the bench and set her tray down. Instead, she leaned toward me and started asking about what Mr. Staley wanted and what I'd done in the first place, at Concord.

"We're not supposed to say," I told her. It felt sort of good to know something that Jackie didn't, for once. Next to me, Maudie cut up her roast beef carefully and started to eat. I hoped she wouldn't come to some gristly part that she'd have to take out with her fingers, in front of everyone.

"Come *on*," Jackie persisted. "I saw you telling Rosemary."

"She didn't say that much," Rosemary put in quickly.

"Well, what *did* you say?" Jackie said. "You were all cracking up before. I thought you were supposed to be in *trouble*."

"We are," Maudie said, patting her hair self-consciously. Jackie's so sharp sometimes, she can make anyone feel awkward. And then, she's so cute and little that you feel big just being near her. Maudie must have felt awfully strained, sitting there. But she kept on. "It isn't funny, really." She glanced up at Rosemary and me and started to smile. "Except, sort of." She looked back down at her plate.

But Jackie wasn't paying attention. She was staring down the aisle between tables. "Look who's coming!" she said in an exaggerated whisper, nudging Christine. "Your true love—Mr. California!"

I looked up. Steve Bader was walking toward us carrying a tray of empty dishes. Billy Taylor was behind him.

Christine poked Jackie's back. "Shut up! He'll *hear* you!"

We all shifted nervously on the bench as the boys came closer. Jackie was trying not to laugh. I fiddled with my milk so they wouldn't catch me staring. Suddenly, Jackie kicked me under the table. I looked up. Steve Bader was standing right beside me!

"Hey, Kate," he said. "How ya doing?"

He hesitated, as though he wanted to say more, but Billy Taylor pushed him along. "Don't stand there gabbing with the girls, Bader."

"Well, see ya," Steve said, looking right at me before he walked away.

"What *is* this, a secret romance?" Jackie looked sort of annoyed.

"Don't ask *me*." I was completely confused. What was *that* all about?

Jackie stood up abruptly. "Boy, nobody can get *anything* out of you these days, Kate." She began to pick up her trash. So did Christine. Then they both climbed over the bench and walked off.

"What do you think Steve wanted?" asked Rosemary.

"I don't know," I said. "Honestly." I wondered if Steve could suddenly have decided I was attractive or something. *That* would be interesting.

The bell rang and we all got up. Maudie turned to us. "Thanks for asking me to eat with you," she said formally. "I had a good time."

We both said, "Oh, sure." Then we hesitated. I was waiting for Rosemary and she was probably waiting for me. We came out with it almost together. "Any time," we said.

Maudie smiled suddenly. She has a really nice smile.

We carried our trays to the trash bins. I looked at the kids grouped around different tables. I didn't know why Maudie would *want* to sit with us, if Jackie and Chris were going to act so snotty. I suddenly wondered why *I* should always sit at the same table. At least every time. I realized that no one was making me. I could sit anywhere I wanted. It might be fun to try different places. Maudie and Rosemary would probably go with me. I decided to bring it up with them before lunch tomorrow.

I crumpled my milk carton, tossed it at the trash can, and made a basket. "Did you see that?" I yelled triumphantly.

It struck me that, for someone in serious trouble, I was feeling pretty cheerful. Maybe it was because of Steve Bader. Maybe from the different tables idea. For practically the first time since I'd been at Revere, the whole thing of friends didn't seem like that much of a problem.

"Come on, guys," I said, and we walked to the door together.

chapter 11

* * *

BUT WHEN I told my parents the whole story at dinner time, I began to realize how serious it was. They were sympathetic to *me*, it wasn't that. But they were both very upset. Mom was furious that anyone would think her daughter would read a dirty book. Dad was more worried about the politics of it.

"A fight over censorship could destroy this town," he said soberly. "That's happened in other communities."

I guess that ever since I was little, I've counted on my parents to tell me things would work out. It scared me that this time neither one of them said that.

Josh looked worried, too. "But why would Mr. Hofsteder take it seriously when they called it a dirty book? That's stupid." He twirled a strand of spaghetti onto his fork.

"It *is* stupid," Mom said quickly. She sighed. "I suppose those parents are just as concerned about their kids as Dad and I are, but attacking a good book is a funny way to show it. Anyway, Mr. Hofsteder would take *any* complaint seriously. He cares how parents feel."

"Then he should care about the ones who would *like* my book," I said quickly. "What about them? They have the right for their kids to hear it."

"Of course they do. Mr. Hofsteder would be the first to agree," Dad said as the phone rang.

Josh looked anxious as Dad reached for it. My parents get mad when Denise calls him up at dinner time.

"Hello? Yes, it is," Dad said, looking irritated. "Millers," he mouthed.

Josh relaxed, but I was annoyed. Why couldn't the Millers ever leave us alone?

"I see." Dad pushed his chair back. "I can understand your position, but I can't agree with it. I'll need more facts before—"

Mr. Miller's voice spluttered loudly through the receiver.

"All I can tell you," Dad said, "is that I'll get back to you as soon as I've got more information. Yes. I understand, Mr. Miller. Good-bye." He slammed the receiver down. "I don't believe it," he said.

"What is it now, Roy?" Mom asked. "Cockroaches? Mice? Flooded basement?"

"Dirty books," said Dad. "It seems that one of the Millers' neighbors' children was exposed to an explicit discussion, led by our daughter, of canine birth. And he's mighty upset about it, let me tell you."

"Oh, *no!*" Mom exclaimed. "That's the last straw!"

"What's their neighbors' child's name?" I asked. Boy. If I'd known that someone connected to the Millers was in Ms. Dwyer's class, I might have been more careful. Still, why should I have been? No matter whose kid was listening, they didn't hear anything *bad*.

"He didn't say." Dad smiled grimly. "Well, Katie, it looks as though you and your teacher are in a tight spot."

"I do wish Ms. Plotkin hadn't rushed into this without thinking," Mom said. "I hate to see Kate suffer for something that's not her responsibility."

"It's not *her* fault," I said quickly. My parents still hadn't met Ms. Plotkin. I really wanted them to like her.

"It's not a question of fault," Dad said, "but she could have planned things better. If only she'd told the school board what was happening." Dad thinks the school board should know everything. That's because of all the years he spent on it.

"Her intentions were fine," Mom said. "She just—"

The phone rang again.

Dad sighed and grabbed the receiver. "Hello," he said shortly. Then he relaxed. "Well. That's nice of you. Yes, she's right here." He handed it to me.

"Hello?" I said nervously.

"This is Marge Robbins, Kate. I'm Alexandra's mother—Alex is in Ms. Dwyer's class."

"Oh, sure." In my mind I pictured Alexandra's cute little face and her pigtails.

"She's been talking about 'the big girls' since your first visit," Mrs. Robbins went on. "You certainly made a big impression. She loved the book you read. She even dragged me to the library to look for it." Her voice turned serious. "But by the time we got there, both copies were out."

"I know," I said quickly. "That's because—"

"Oh, I don't want to get started on *that*," Mrs. Robbins interrupted. What I'm calling to ask is—you must have lots of people asking, but would you be available to baby-sit? We have theater tickets for Saturday, and we just found out our regular sitter isn't free that night."

"Oh, I'd *love* to," I said. "Only, there's this thing—" I'd better explain if she didn't know. "Some people thought that book I read was bad for their kids."

"I know some parents are stirring up trouble," Mrs. Robbins said. "But I talked to Ms. Dwyer, and I trust her opinion. She spoke very highly of you, Kate. And Alex is so taken with you—that's really the most important thing."

"Thanks," I said. It was hard to act cool with Mom and Dad smiling dotingly at me. "There's one other thing," I added, hating to admit it. "I'm only eleven, and I never baby-sat before. I wanted to, but so far no one's asked."

"Well, I'm asking," said Mrs. Robbins easily. "So, if you're free—"

"Oh, *sure!*"

Mrs. Robbins explained how to get to their house. "I'm so eager to meet you," she said, before she hung up.

I put the receiver down and raised my arms like a champ. "I'm a baby-sitter! Me!"

Mom jumped up and hugged me. "Congratulations, hon. That's wonderful."

The phone rang again.

This time Josh grabbed it, but it still wasn't Denise. He gave the receiver to Mom. "It's Ms. Plotkin."

Ms. Plotkin!

"Of course," Mom was saying. "Fine. We'll be pleased to meet you. See you then." She handed the receiver back to Josh. "Ms. Plotkin's going to drop by," she said. "They've been having a small meeting about this situation and she wants to fill us in. Turn on the porch light, will you, Kate?"

"What *kind* of meeting?" I asked.

"The people most involved," Mom said. "Ms. Plotkin and Ms. Dwyer, Gerda, Mr. Hofsteder, Mr. Staley." She began to rummage in the breadbox. "There was a big pack of cookies in here, and it's vanished!"

"It was Josh," I said quickly. "I hardly got one."

"Hardly," Josh said. "More like twenty-one."

"*Josh!*"

"Cut it out, kids," said Mom absently. "I'll just

make some fresh coffee—" Mom would fuss over company if they were coming to tell her the *world* was ending.

The phone rang.

"What a night!" Dad answered it. "Yes, he is." He gave it to Josh. "The one you've been waiting for."

"Oh, *hi*," Josh said in that dumb tone he uses for Denise. "Wait till I go to the upstairs phone." He gave me the receiver. "Hang up when I tell you."

"What'll you give me?" I asked, but Josh was already halfway up the stairs. "Mom, don't fuss a lot, will you," I said, holding the receiver. "And don't, you know, start telling Ms. Plotkin how wonderful I am—"

"Hang *up*, wonderful," Josh's voice came through the phone.

I slammed it down.

The doorbell rang.

"I'll get it!" I ran to the door. Ms. Plotkin stood there stamping off her boots.

"Come on in." Suddenly I felt shy. It's always strange to see teachers away from school. They seem more like regular people. When Ms. Plotkin took off her coat, she was wearing a print blouse I'd never seen before. It was pretty.

Mom and Dad came into the hall, and I introduced them. Right away, they started saying those polite things parents and teachers have to say when they meet each other.

"Kate's such a pleasure to have in class," Ms. Plotkin began, following Mom into the living room.

"Well, she just *raves* about you," Mom said back.

I shot her a warning look. I didn't want Ms. Plotkin to think she was that dopey kind of mother.

"So," said Dad, sitting down. "I gather some folks are getting worked up about the book Kate read at Concord." At least he didn't start right in about how she should have told the school board.

"They are," Ms. Plotkin said, arranging a couch pillow behind her. "But don't worry, Kate," she said to me. "After tonight's meeting, I think things will work out." She smiled nervously.

Then she began to tell about the meeting. It had been at the library. Mr. Staley had brought the copy of the book he'd borrowed from Mrs. Bergen that afternoon. "Everyone thought it was very appropriate for first-grade children," Ms. Plotkin said. "Mrs. Brooks brought four book reviews of it with her, all of them highly positive. She said she was shocked that anyone would complain about it. But then Gerda told us that a woman had come into the library this afternoon and said it was a crime to spend public funds on smut like that!"

I almost snickered. I've always thought "smut" was a disgusting word. But the idea that anyone would use it for an innocent book like *The Birthday Dog* wasn't funny. It was infuriating.

"That's dumb!" I said.

"It's serious," said Dad. "This could blow up into a big censorship fight." He looked sternly at Ms. Plotkin. It suddenly seemed as though *he* was the teacher and she was a child who'd done something wrong. "I hope you made some plans for calming things down, tonight," he said.

"Oh, yes," Ms. Plotkin said quickly. "The first thing was to write an article for the *Crier*, describing the project." She broke off. "I'm ashamed that we didn't do that before we started. I mentioned it to Mr. Staley, but I think he wanted to be sure Anne Dwyer and I could make a success of the project before we wrote about it publicly."

Poor Ms. Plotkin—Mr. Staley didn't seem to have much faith in her. I guess because she was new and inexperienced. He should have realized what a good teacher she was. I hoped Dad did.

"Mr. Staley's public relations sense isn't very acute, I'm afraid," Dad said wryly. "He might have avoided all this if he'd let the board in on it from the start."

"And got some parents involved, so they'd know what was going on," Mom said.

"Oh, we made some plans to do that, at the meeting tonight," Ms. Plotkin said eagerly. "Anne and Mrs. Brooks are going to have a meeting for first-grade parents, about books for young children."

"That's a good idea," Mom said approvingly.

"And Gerda's planning a series of meetings at the library," Ms. Plotkin went on. "She's going to work up a list of good books for children, including some controversial ones, and invite parents from my class and anyone else who's interested to discuss them together."

"I'd like to do that!" Mom said. "Children's books

have changed so much since I was a girl. I feel as though I don't know anything about them."

"They've changed since I grew up, too," said Ms. Plotkin. "Well, *times* have changed. And kids."

I hoped they weren't going to get off on a discussion of Youth Today. I hate it when adults do that in front of you.

"Small meetings are a good idea," Dad said, getting back to the subject. "It's better to avoid a big public meeting. I just hope nobody gets the idea of bringing the project up before the board right now. Issues of censorship are much too complex to settle in an angry shouting match."

Actually, Dad *likes* complex issues. It's part of his political-mindedness. He can go on for hours about a subject like freedom of speech. It's interesting, but sometimes Josh and I might rather be watching TV or something.

Mom jumped up. "Oh, I forgot the coffee!"

The phone rang.

"I'll get it!" Josh yelled down. Then he called, "It's for Ms. Plotkin."

Mom took her to the kitchen phone. "She seems like such a nice person," she said to Dad, as she came back. "It's too bad that a young, enthusiastic teacher should get burned like this—"

"Enthusiasm's not enough," Dad said grimly. "A little more advice and support from Mr. Staley would have helped." Then he relaxed a bit. "Still, she seems sensible as well as lively. I think you're lucky to have her, Kate."

"Oh, I am!" I was relieved that they weren't going to blame everything on her.

Ms. Plotkin came back looking tense. "That was Mr. Staley," she said. "He took our letter over to the *Crier* office just now. The editor told him that he'd had some very angry letters about the project and Kate's book. They'll be in the paper tomorrow."

Oh, man. Now the whole town would get worked up!

"That's bad news," Dad said. "I'm glad your article will be in the paper with them."

"I hope it will help," said Ms. Plotkin. "Now, I should go. Tomorrow's going to be a full day. Oh, Kate, I meant to ask if I could borrow your copy of the book. I'd like to read it aloud in class."

"Sure." I ran upstairs to get it. On the way down I stared at the picture on the cover. That little puppy looked so sweet and innocent! If he only knew.

"I completely forgot the coffee," Mom was saying in the hall.

But Ms. Plotkin said she shouldn't stay. "It's been so nice to meet you," she told my parents. "Thanks for your support."

Mom and Dad said they were glad to meet *her*. I knew they meant it, so that was good. It's awful for kids when your parents don't get along with your teachers or vice versa. You feel stuck in the middle.

After Ms. Plotkin left, I went upstairs to tell Josh about the letters to the *Crier*. His door was closed. I knocked and he opened it, looking cross.

"Guess what?" I said. "All these people wrote angry

letters to the paper and they're going to print them tomorrow."

"Guess what?" Josh said right back.

"What?"

"Denise's *father* wrote one. Denise is all worked up about it. She doesn't want me to go over there for a while. She says it would be too embarrassing, because our parents are on different sides. So—" he shrugged. "For now, the romance is off."

He was trying to sound cool, but I knew he was upset.

"Oh, *Josh!*" I stood there stupidly as he closed the door slowly in my face. Did he think it was *my* fault?

I wondered what could happen next.

chapter 12

* * *

I WOULD NEVER have predicted the first thing that happened. Steve Bader came up to me outside school the next morning and started this long conversation!

It turned out that some angry parent had called Steve's mother the night before to "alert" her to "disturbing trends" in the schools. This woman said that young children had been exposed to explicit sex materials and that reading lists for older kids were full of what she called trash. She wanted the Baders to come to a meeting at her house last night, where parents who stood for "clean, character-building literature" were going to start a campaign for decent books.

"That's not fair!" I said, too angry to be shy with

OCT 5 – DEC 9
TICKETS $10–$15

CORDUROY

CORDUROY
Based on the *Corduroy* and *A Pocket for Corduroy* books by Don Freeman
Licensed by CBS Consumer Products
Adapted for Stage by Barry Kornhauser
Directed by Allison Watrous
Education Partners: Margot & Allan Frank and Alan & Carol Meny

DENVER CENTER FOR THE
PERFORMING ARTS
Education

Bring your Pre-K through 3rd graders to **join in this beloved, classic adventure**

Join Corduroy the teddy bear on his delightfully rollicking chase through every section of the department store in search of his missing button. Bring your Pre-K through 3rd graders to this tender, enduring story of true friendship as it stirs up the stage!

Steve. "Who are *they* to decide what's decent or not?"

"That's just what Mom said," Steve said quickly. "She told this Mrs. Bergen that she wouldn't come to her meeting because, in the first place, she hadn't read the book they were complaining about, so she couldn't judge it, and in the second place she *had* read some of the books my sister and I brought home and she thought they were excellent." Steve grinned. "So then Mrs. Bergen said Mom should ask us about the books we *didn't* show her. She said Mom would probably find out we were reading smut behind her back."

"Smut—that's what someone called the book I read to the kids at Concord!" Like a dope, I started to giggle. It just suddenly struck me as ridiculous that my first real conversation with Steve Bader should be about smut.

All around us, kids were running up the walks. It was nearly time for the bell, but Steve kept on.

"Back in California last year there was this big fight over a book my sister's teacher put on the eighth-grade reading list," Steve went on. "Some people thought it was a bad book. The woman who called Mom last night sounded just like them."

So *that* was why Steve had wanted to talk to me. I felt sort of dumb for thinking it was my looks or personality. Still, I was glad he cared about the problem. I wouldn't be interested in any boy who didn't have opinions.

"What book were they upset about?" I asked.

"Anne Frank's diary."

"*I* read that! It's the saddest, most beautiful book I've ever read," I said. "Why would anyone complain about *it?*"

"They said it had bad language or something. Some people even tried to get the teacher fired for recommending it. Mom worked on a committee to support her. They won, in the end. But it was crazy for a while. People were rushing to school and pulling books off the shelves, just to look for dirty words in them so they could prove how bad the teacher was. They even complained about the dictionary!"

"You're kidding!"

"No, honestly. Because it has words like 'bed' and stuff." Steve grinned in an embarrassed way.

"Some people would complain about anything," I said, trying to sound cool.

"Hey, Kate!"

I turned. Jackie was waving at me from the path. She looked as though she wanted to come over, but I waved back as though I didn't expect her to.

"You'd better come in, Harris. It's time for the bell," she said, standing on the bottom step. I knew she was trying to get Steve's attention.

But he had started to rummage around in his notebook. "I'd better go," he said. "I promised to give Taylor some notes before class. Hang in there, Kate. It'll be O.K. in the end." He tapped my shoulder and went off.

"What'd *he* want?" Jackie hurried over.

"Nothing. We were just talking about stuff." I was glad she'd seen me there with him.

The bell rang.

"Come on," I said. "We'd better hurry up."

Jackie followed me to my locker. "You've got to tell me what's going on," she said. "I tried to call you last night, but your line was busy for hours."

"I know. Everyone was calling. About a book I read at Concord." I wondered how much she knew by now.

"Some woman called Mom last night," Jackie said right away, "and tried to get her to come to this meeting about dirty books. Mom said the woman was practically hysterical. She kept complaining about the book you read at Concord. What was *in* it, anyway?"

"It was about this *puppy*." I was beginning to feel sort of tired of this. "Mrs. Bergen got people to write letters to the *Crier* about it. About me, too, I guess."

"Hey, you'll be famous!" Jackie said. We had come to my locker. I dialed the combination, but the lock stuck.

"I certainly didn't ask to be," I said, tugging at it. If you're the least bit nervous, it never works. I clicked it back to zero and started over. "You'd better get your stuff, Jackie—you'll be late."

Jackie looked as though she wanted to ask me more, but then ran off. "See you in English."

I almost wished I didn't have to go to English. Telling the whole story one more time would be exhausting. And then, I didn't know how people would react. I walked slowly to Ms. Plotkin's room. As soon as I went in, kids came over.

"Hey, Harris, I heard you got into trouble!"

"Did you really read a dirty book at Concord?"

It looked as though I was already famous. I didn't like it.

Maudie was standing across the room with a bunch of kids around her. It was ironic how everyone wanted to talk to her now. If you ask me, they should have apologized for treating her like a pariah before. She looked up, and I pointed to two seats near Rosemary. We made our way over and sat down.

"Kate, are you O.K.?" Rosemary asked. "Mom got this awful phone call about you last night. She was furious with the woman who called—somebody named Mrs. Bergen."

"Mrs. Bergen sure gets around," I said.

"There're a million rumors this morning," Maudie said excitedly.

"Hey, kids," Ms. Plotkin called. "Take your seats, will you? We have a lot to talk about today."

People looked at Maudie and me.

Ms. Plotkin got up. "A lot of rumors are spreading through school," she said, "and the best way to stop them is with facts. I'm going to tell you the facts I know, as impartially as I can, and then we'll see what we can learn from them." She pulled some notes out of a desk drawer. "Kate and Maudie and I have become involved in a very crucial issue, one that affects all of us in this room, and this school, and this town." She paused to smile at Maudie and me.

"It all began," she said, "right here in this room, on that day last month when I asked for volunteers for a reading project at Concord School, and Kate and Maudie raised their hands."

The room was absolutely still. Ms. Plotkin held up *The Birthday Dog* and read it straight through, and then passed it around so everyone could see the illustrations. When she repeated what the little kids said after the story, a few kids snickered. Honestly. Some people act like babies.

As she talked, kids raised their hands and burst out with questions, but Ms. Plotkin asked them not to interrupt her till she finished. She spoke very calmly. I happened to look at the clock when she got to the end. It had taken her twenty minutes just to tell all the facts.

"Now, then," she said. "Your assignment for today will be to read everything on this topic in the *Crier* when you get home. Read thoughtfully!" She pushed back her chair. "I think we should let Kate begin our discussion, if she wants to, and Maudie can fill in after that."

I didn't know what to add, she'd explained things so well. "I don't have much more to say," I began. "Just, it's not *fair!*" I was surprised to hear my voice rising. "I thought it was a good book when I picked it out, and I still do. I chose it because one kid in Ms. Dwyer's class said he had a new puppy, and I thought he'd like it. It sort of hurts my feelings the way everyone jumped on me as though I was some kind of monster. I'm not!" I took a breath. "I'm not a sex maniac, either!" I added. Then I blushed. I hadn't expected to say *that* in public.

But hardly anyone laughed.

"No, you're not," Ms. Plotkin said. She was smiling. "That's absolutely right. Maudie?"

"First of all," Maudie said, starting right in as though she'd planned a speech, "I agree with Kate. And then—what makes me mad is that the idea of the project was so good, and honestly, the kids at Concord really liked us. They're probably wondering why we can't come back, and I don't know how Ms. Dwyer can explain it to them. It doesn't seem right for *them* to be punished just because some people are afraid of an innocent book." She stopped abruptly, pushed her hair off her face, and looked around with a shy smile. I don't think she'd ever said that much in class before. For no reason, it suddenly occurred to me that I'd stopped thinking of her as fat.

"Thank you, Maudie," Ms. Plotkin said. "Who'd like to add something?"

Steve raised his hand. "The whole issue is freedom of speech," he said seriously. "I think people should be free to say what they want to, and read what they want."

"Read anything?" Ms. Plotkin asked him seriously. "That's something I always worry about when I'm assigning books. I agree with you in one part of my mind, but the truth is that there are some books I really wish you kids wouldn't read until you're older and you've had more experience. So I think I can understand how parents must feel."

Nobody said anything. I guess none of us wanted to admit that we weren't very experienced. Still, I sort of knew what she meant.

"Of course, the children at Concord are a special case," Ms. Plotkin went on, "because they have to be read *to*. It's a big responsibility to choose books that they'll understand and enjoy and learn something from." She looked at me. "I happen to think *The Birthday Dog is* that kind of book, but obviously some people don't."

Tony Marcus raised his hand. "My mother says there are certain things little children should learn at home from their parents, not in school."

"But what if your parents don't tell you?" Billy Taylor burst in. "I mean, kids ought to know about how dogs get born and stuff. If their parents won't tell them, what's wrong with hearing it from a book?"

"That's what I think," Jackie said. "It's not fair for parents to keep certain books from kids just because *they're* embarrassed."

"It's not only embarrassment that makes parents protective," said Ms. Plotkin. "It's real concern for their kids. Children are exposed to so many terrible things on TV—and in real life!—that parents can't control. It's natural for them to want to have a say about the books their kids read."

That seemed reasonable. "But they should at least *read* the books before they try to censor them," I said quickly. "They shouldn't get hysterical just because someone *else* says they're dirty."

"Or call a whole book bad just because they don't like one little thing about it," Steve added.

"That's a good point," said Ms. Plotkin. "We should always look at a *whole* book—the theme and the style and the author's intentions, all those things that we've talked about this semester—before we judge it." She looked seriously at us. "Of course, people will always have different opinions. Look at the way we've disagreed about some books on our own reading list. But I think you kids are learning to criticize books thoughtfully—"

She broke off as a messenger from the office came in to give her a slip of paper. She read it to herself, biting her lip. Then she looked up.

"I'd hoped this wouldn't happen," she said. "But a public meeting of the school board has been called for Thursday night. Some parents have asked them to vote on whether our project should continue."

People gasped. Maudie reached over and grabbed my arm. We looked at each other. What if they stopped it for good?

The bell rang.

"Wait a minute, kids," Ms. Plotkin said as we grabbed our things. "Don't forget, I want all of you to read today's *Crier* when you get home. I hope you'll talk these issues over with your parents. And I think it would be a good idea if you went to the school board meeting with them, too." She smiled briefly. "O.K.—that's it for today."

She looked so worried that I went up and took her hand. "It'll be all right, Ms. Plotkin."

"Thanks, Kate. Sure it will." She didn't sound that sure.

It was scary how *fast* everything was happening.

Anyway, at lunch time a good thing happened. Maudie and Rosemary and I went through the cafeteria line together. When we got to the end of it we noticed Billy and Steve and some other boys waving to us from their table. So we went over and sat down with them. I think that was the first time any kids in our grade ate lunch with the opposite sex. It was neat.

chapter 13

* * *

WHEN I turned onto my street that afternoon, the paper girl had just tossed our *Crier* on our porch and was riding down the street, throwing papers as she went. She has a pretty good aim. Watching her, I thought of all the people who were going to open up their *Crier* in the next few hours and find angry letters about me in it.

I stopped at the mailbox at the end of our driveway and looked in. I don't usually get mail, but I always think I might. This time, I had a letter. It was a square envelope that looked like an invitation, addressed in handwriting I didn't recognize. I wondered if someone was inviting me to a party. That would be terrific. It wasn't *that* unlikely—if Steve Bader could ask me to sit at his lunch table out of the blue, he might also have invited me to a party. Feeling sort of excited, I walked up the steps and picked up the *Crier* and unlocked the door. I dumped the mail and the paper on the kitchen table, poured out a glass of milk and unpeeled a banana, trying to make the expectation last. Then I opened the envelope.

Boy. I don't know why I never remember about Dr. Klingman's check-up notices. They fool me every time. "According to our records," the card I pulled out said, "it has been six months since your last visit to this office." I threw the envelope in the trash and tacked the notice to the bulletin board. There's no point in throwing it away—Dr. Klingman's office will just keep sending you new ones. For spite, I hunted up an old Milky Way bar I'd hidden from Josh in the back of a cupboard drawer. If I had to get my teeth cleaned anyway, I might as well give Dr. Klingman something to scrape off.

I could practically feel the sugar attacking my tooth enamel as I opened the *Crier* to the Letters column. I glanced over it quickly. All the letters were about the project. They were all against it.

Mrs. Bergen's was the worst. It had one sentence about "innocent sixth-grade children being required to describe reproduction." Then it went on about how moral values were being corrupted by smut. At the end it asked for "decent, character-building materials in our schools and libraries."

That letter shouldn't have bothered me. Anyone who read it could see Mrs. Bergen didn't know the facts, and that she was using what Dad calls "emotionally-charged language" to cover up her fuzzy thinking. But it really got me mad. It was bad enough for her to imply that Maudie and I were immoral, but it was just infuriating the way she made us sound like dopes. "Innocent sixth-grade children," *honestly!*

The next two letters were practically identical. They used almost the same words, including, naturally, "smut." The people who wrote them must have gotten together and copied from Mrs. Bergen. I was glad the editor had printed them next to each other, to show up how un-original they were.

I wished I could just laugh at them, but I couldn't. Those dumb letters hurt my feelings. Whoever made up the poem about "sticks and stones" was wrong. Words do hurt you.

The next letter had a more reasonable tone. It didn't mention "smut" or anything. It said that the project was carelessly planned, and that people should have been told about it before it started. It talked about "inexperienced teachers." That would hurt Ms. Plotkin.

In a way, the last letter was the worst. First of all, it was from Denise's father. And then, it made me wonder for the first time if maybe I *had* done something wrong. This is what it said:

Of course, all children must learn the facts of reproduction. But I believe that no child should be exposed to them until he or she is ready. And it is impossible for even the most well-meaning teacher to know when the moment is right for every child in the class. That is why my wife and I believe that the home is the only appropriate place for books about sex or reproduction.

In a way I had to agree with what Mr. McConnell said. It *would* be wrong to shock little children with facts they weren't ready for. I'd feel awful if I'd done that to any of Ms. Dwyer's kids. But then—I couldn't see how *The Birthday Dog* was shocking. I wondered if Mr. McConnell had actually read the book. Maybe he was just jumping to conclusions.

But his letter wasn't hysterical and stupid. There was no reason for Denise to be ashamed of her father for writing it. He was only saying what he believed. I suddenly wished I had some way to say what *I* believed. For a second, I imagined myself making a speech at the board meeting. But I couldn't do that. I'd be too embarrassed.

Then I remembered about Ms. Plotkin's article. I turned the page and found the headline: INNOVATIVE READING PROGRAM BEGINS AT CONCORD SCHOOL. The article began with statements from the two principals. Mr. Staley's was sort of long-winded but Mr. Hofsteder's was nice. It explained that both little kids and older ones can learn a lot from working together. I had certainly learned a lot already! There was a sentence about Maudie and me. It called us "outstanding students." I hoped Mrs. Bergen would read *that*. Then there was a short description of *Little Bear* and *The Birthday Dog*, which mentioned the birth scene in a matter-of-fact way. The last sentence was neat.

"Asked for his opinion of the project, six-year-old Simon Brady summed it up. 'I love the big girls,' he said. 'They're good teachers.' "

The whole article made the project sound sensible and good, the way it actually was. But it made the angry letters seem even more infuriating. How could they say such terrible things about something so educational? It wasn't *fair!*

To calm myself down, I read all the funnies and Ann Landers and Hints from Heloise. I even read the Pattern of the Day, which was for a stupid crotcheted poncho. Then I went to the phone and dialed Maudie's number.

"Weren't you *furious* about those letters?" she said right away.

"Yeah. I'd like to tell that Mrs. Bergen a thing or two," I said.

"You ought to," Maudie said quickly. "You should get up and say what you think at the school board meeting. You really should."

"Are you kidding?" It was funny she'd thought of the same thing. "I couldn't, Maudie. Honestly. I'd die."

Maudie didn't say anything. I wondered if she thought I was chicken or something. "There'd be all those parents looking at me," I said, defensively. "And Mr. Staley, and the teachers. Kids in our *class!*" I couldn't imagine myself standing up in front of all those people, much less going into what had happened. "Maudie, listen—*I'd* have to say all those words the *kids* said, and how could I do that? It was bad enough just telling Mr. Staley!"

Maudie laughed. "You probably wouldn't have to. But you could practice ahead of time. Just say every embarrassing word that might come up over and over in your head, and after a while they wouldn't even bother you."

I knew what she meant. If you say the same words often enough, the meaning seems to fade away. "I did that once with 'bubble gum,' when I was little," I told her. "I was opening a pack of it and for some reason I started saying the words a lot of times and the whole meaning of them vanished."

"Bubble gum, bubble gum, bubble gum," Maudie said thoughtfully. "Hey, it works!" She giggled. "So—you could say anything, if you practiced. No kidding, Kate. It would be so *good* if you talked back to Mrs. Bergen. You might be able to save the whole *project!*"

"Well—" I *hate* to make speeches.

"Think about it!" Maudie broke off. One of her sisters was saying something in the background. "I have to go," she said. "I promised to read to Andrea."

"Be sure to pick a decent book."

"Ha!" Maudie said. "See you tomorrow. Don't forget—practice!"

Feeling sort of trapped, I went to the hall and stared into the mirror. I wondered if I *could* make a speech in public. I'd probably feel proud of myself, if I did. I made a face at my reflection.

"Penis," I said to it, tentatively. "Penis. Pe—"

The front door opened and Josh walked in.

"Oh, hi," I said weakly. "I was just—"

Josh went right into the kitchen. "Where's the paper?"

"On the table. Mr. McConnell's letter wasn't that bad, Josh. Honestly. Some of the other ones are awful. But I practically agree with what Mr. Mc—"

"Shut up and let me *read!*" Josh shouted.

"You don't have to be *rude* about it," I yelled back. I had enough on my mind without him. I was pretty sure I wouldn't make the speech, after all. I'd probably get too emotional.

Josh came out holding the paper.

"So?" I asked.

"It's not bad," he said stiffly. "Compared to Mrs. Bergen's, and those other people's."

"That's what I was trying to *tell* you."

"Yeah. But what I'm trying to tell *you* is, Denise is still going to be upset. She thinks our parents are so wonderful and liberal compared to hers. She says she'll be ashamed to show her face after people see her father's letter. She's not even speaking to her father. She has this stupid idea that our parents' ideas have to keep us apart, like Romeo and Juliet or something." He looked embarrassed.

"Well, if she's going to act that stupid about it, why don't you get yourself a different girl friend?" I asked reasonably. I wouldn't mind. Then Josh wouldn't have to spend all his time down at the harbor.

"Why don't you just shut up?" he shot back

110

furiously. "If you hadn't got into all this in the first place—" He started up the stairs.

"Why don't *you* shut up," I said back. People act so self-centered when they're in love. They don't consider anyone else's feelings.

I went out to the kitchen and opened the freezer. There was a package of chicken and one of pork chops. I pulled the pork chops out to thaw. Let Josh suffer from the smell. It would serve him right.

A car door slammed outside. Mom came in and plonked down on a chair.

"Hi, Mom," I said. "You should hear what Josh—"

"Oh, what *now?*" She sounded so tired I felt scared.

"Is something the matter?" I asked, as Dad came in, looking grim.

"Roy and I had kind of a setback this afternoon," Mom said wearily.

"What happened?"

"It seems that while the Liebermans were waiting for us to take them to the lawyer's office, to draw up their mortgage contract—" Mom broke off. "They're that nice couple we told you about, who wanted to buy the house on Shore Road? Well, while they were waiting for Dad and me they bought a copy of the *Crier* to get a feel of what Sussex is like—"

"And they saw the letters? And they don't want to buy the house, because of *me!*" I yelled. "Oh, Mom!"

"That's not it, Katie," said Dad. "It's just the opposite. The Liebermans were worried about the bitterness in some of those letters. They thought it over and decided they shouldn't be hasty about

111

settling in a town where people could react so angrily over a censorship issue. They're going to have a baby soon, and they want their child to go to school in an open atmosphere." He patted my shoulder. "They've decided to take another week to think it over, that's all."

"Oh, Dad," I cried out. "It seems like everything's going wrong. I wish I'd never even heard of Ms. Plotkin's stupid project!" I felt tears in my eyes. I brushed at them angrily.

"Kate," said Mom. "Think of your baby-sitting job. Think—"

"I'm *tired* of thinking!" I yelled and ran upstairs and threw myself down on my bed and cried.

chapter 14

* * *

MOM HAS this saying, "Things always get worse before they get better." I don't see why they always *should* have to, but in this case they certainly did. The next afternoon—it was Wednesday, the day before the board meeting—she and I had driven to the Shore Acres Mall to do grocery shopping. It was late in the day, and the sky was already dark. When we got out of the car the wind whipped at our faces and practically pushed us across the parking lot. It was the kind of weather that makes you wish for summer, when you can do errands like a free human being without struggling through the wind in pounds of heavy clothes.

I grabbed a basket that came rolling toward us and we headed for the A & P. There were some people huddled around a table in front of it, under the shelter of the roof. You often see people there having bake sales or selling chances for charity or something, but it seemed unusual for these people to be doing it in the dark and the cold. I thought they were very noble to be so dedicated to whatever cause they were working for.

But then, when I dragged the shopping cart up the curb, I read the hand-lettered sign fastened to the front of their table. It said PARENTS UNITED FOR DECENCY!

A woman with a heavy scarf over most of her face poked a sheet of paper in front of Mom's face. "Good evening," she said through the wool. "We're recruiting concerned parents for a new organization, Parents United for Decency. Won't you sign up and join us?"

Hastily, I pulled the cart toward the IN door, praying that Mom was following me. But when I glanced back, Mom was still standing there, holding the paper in her gloved hand. There were two other women huddled behind the table. All three of them had their eyes fixed on Mom.

"Mom," I said nervously, edging closer to the door. Why didn't she come *on?*

But Mom stood there, reading the paper. Finally she looked up. "I'm sorry," she said in an ominous tone to the woman who had given it to her. "I didn't get your name?"

"Judith Bergen," the woman said. "Mrs. *Henry* Bergen."

Mrs. Bergen!

Mom didn't step back. "I'm Nina Harris," she said

firmly. "Now—just what is it that your group hopes to do?"

"Mom!" I said again, more urgently. Any minute, those women were going to figure out who I was. I stepped back and the IN door swung open behind me, letting out a blast of warm air. I was tempted to duck inside and hide among the bright, deserted aisles. But I couldn't just leave Mom standing there.

"We're organizing a campaign to keep filthy reading materials—books that subvert wholesome values—out of our children's schools and libraries," Mrs. Bergen was saying. "We've already pressured the school board to hold a public meeting on this dreadful new project where innocent children—"

She broke off as a woman followed by a little child pushed her shopping cart through the OUT door. "Come, Billy," the woman said, pulling the child away from Mrs. Bergen's table. "Billy! Come on!" Grabbing his arm firmly with one hand and guiding the cart with the other, she hurried toward the parked cars. You could see she was trying to avoid the women at the table. They'd probably given her a hard time on her way in.

Mrs. Bergen turned back to Mom. "You've probably heard," she said, "that only last week the little first-grade children at Concord School were subjected to a book that displayed a birth scene in explicit detail. And that's only the tip of the iceberg—"

"*Mom!*" I said helplessly. If she'd just come *in* before the women found out. But Mom didn't budge. I should have known. She'll never back away from an argument when she thinks the other person is wrong or is hurting one of her children, and in this case both those things were true. Looking at her, wrapped in her bulky coat, I suddenly remembered how when I was little she used to remind me of a mother bear defending her cubs. It could be scary when she got enraged, like the time when she stormed into the school lunch room and scolded the cafeteria aide who'd forced me to finish my hamburger when, as it turned out, I was starting to get measles. But no matter how embarrassing her protectiveness might be, it was comforting, too. I always felt safe, knowing that she'd stick up for me.

Mom was enraged now, I knew. And even though I was scared and embarrassed, I was glad that she was standing up to Mrs. Bergen.

"I think you're very wrong," she said, handing the paper back. "You've blown this issue all out of proportion. As it happens, I've read the book you're talking about, and I think it's a *good* book—it's warm and direct and truthful. I trust the professional judgment of the teachers and librarians who recommended it. *And*," she drew herself up dramatically, pointing to me, "this is my daughter, Kate, who read that book to the children at Concord."

The women gasped. I forced myself to look them in the eye.

"Oh, well, then," Mrs. Bergen said sharply. "Naturally, you'd be prejudiced—"

"I think *you're* prejudiced," Mom shot back. "I think

it's a sad day for this community when a little group of parents would take it upon themselves to stand in judgment on all the rest of us who support our teachers. And our librarians. My second cousin once-removed happens to be the children's librarian—" Mom paused as a car drove past in a clank of tire chains. One of the women behind the table jerked at Mrs. Bergen's coat sleeve. "I think—" she said nervously.

But I knew there would be no stopping Mom. Now she was going to defend Gerda, as well as me.

"My second cousin once-removed," Mom said loudly, "graduated at the top of her class in library school, and she personally recommended this book to my daughter. I'll take her professional opinion any day over the misinformed ranting of people who don't know a wholesome book when they read one. *If* some of them have even read it!" Abruptly, she turned away, leaving the women gaping at her. "Kate. Let's go in."

Quickly, I pushed the cart through the door. We skirted a table of grapefruit and stopped in front of the apple bins.

"I can't believe it!" Mom leaned wearily against the display. "What next?"

"You were good, Mom," I said. I wished I'd had the nerve to speak up, too.

Mom smiled a little. "I guess I got sort of worked up. But it makes me so mad! To think this should happen in *Sussex*, of all places! Why, this town was *settled* by people who came here so they could speak freely!" She tugged her gloves off and threw them into the cart.

"I know it." Aunt Lucy's always talking about that. The settlers were our ancestors.

Mom put a bag of apples in the cart. "I just hate to have to go home and tell Roy about this, when he's already worried about the board meeting."

"Were there lots of names on that paper?" I asked, poking at the bananas. They were all like rocks.

"No!" Mom relaxed a bit. "Only five or six. I can't believe they'll find many people to join them before tomorrow night. Most people would want to get the whole story at the meeting *before* they signed up."

"I bet the Millers would sign."

"They probably will!" Mom said, wryly. "The Millers don't wait for the facts before *they* complain." She put two bags of alfalfa sprouts in the cart and we went on to the deli counter.

"I'll have half a pound of Swiss," Mom said. "And—"

"Mrs. *Harris!*" said somebody behind us. "And Kate—I'm so glad to bump into you both!"

It was Mrs. Bader, and Steve was with her! He grinned at me.

"What do you make of those people outside?" asked Mrs. Bader breathlessly. "They must be the same group who were making phone calls last night. I can't believe this is happening in Sussex—" Then she began to tell Mom the whole story of the censorship fight in California.

Steve and I stood there and listened. It was

interesting, but I would sort of rather have talked to Steve. He looked as though he felt the same way, but I guess neither of us felt like interrupting our mothers. It's funny how hard it is to act natural sometimes, in front of them.

"Will there be anything else?" asked the deli man, trying to get Mom's attention.

"Oh, yes. Sorry." She began to order lunch meat.

Mrs. Bader turned to me. "Steve says he's so pleased to be in English with you," she said.

Steve looked flustered. I wondered if he'd actually ever said that. The trouble with mothers' remarks is that you can never be quite sure. They tend to exaggerate.

"Ms. Plotkin sounds like a wonderful teacher," Mrs. Bader went on. "I do hope this project of hers can continue. I've told Steve it would be great if he could get into it." She looked meaningfully at Steve. I wondered if she'd been pressuring him about it.

The deli man handed Mom's package over the counter and she turned to us. "Isn't it nice that you're in a class together." A familiar look was coming over her face. I had a sudden premonition that she might actually ask him over to visit! I don't think she realizes that in sixth grade mothers should never do that, especially with a boy.

"Mom," I said, to head her off. "It's sort of late."

But Mrs. Bader was smiling dotingly at me. "You must come over and visit us, Kate," she said, right out of the blue. "It would be lovely for Steven."

Poor Steve! Then he surprised me. "Why don't

* 119

you?" he asked. "You could walk home with me after school some day."

"Sure," I said, as cool as I could. Wait till I told Maudie about *that!*

Then we headed down different aisles and finished our shopping. By the time we got to the check-out counter, the women at the table had gone away. But I knew I hadn't seen the last of them. They'd all be at the board meeting the next night.

chapter 15

* * *

THE DAY of the meeting started badly. I woke up freezing and stiff because my covers had slipped off and my bedroom's always cold because Dad turns the thermostat way down at night. Outside the windows, it was a cold, dull day, the kind that reminds you winter's going to hang in there for months.

At breakfast, my parents kept trying to say cheerful things, which made me feel grimmer. Josh spooned up his oatmeal without saying a word. He was probably rehearsing what he'd say to Denise. I didn't feel like eating. I hoped Mom wouldn't notice, but of course she did.

"Have some oatmeal, Katie," she said. "You want something hot in your stomach on a cold day like this."

That was just what I *didn't* want, but I ate the

oatmeal. It joggled in my stomach all the way to school.

Maudie was waiting for me at my locker. "So," she said in an excited way. "This is the big day. Did you practice?"

"Practice what?"

"You know. For your speech."

"Oh, Maudie, I don't know if I can do it!" I began telling her about Mrs. Bergen and the others at the A & P. "Mom was so terrific, no kidding, but I just stood there like a drip."

"Yeah, but that was worse in a way," Maudie said. "I mean, you weren't *expecting* them. The shock of it probably got to you. But at the meeting, there'll be all these people rooting for you."

" 'All these people' is part of the problem," I argued. "They'll all be staring at me!"

We had come to the door of Ms. Plotkin's room. Everyone was talking in little groups but when they saw us they looked up and started to come over. It suddenly reminded me of going into the room at Concord, and I felt sad.

But the kids were nice. They all started talking about the meeting, and how their parents were coming, and that the board would never vote against the project.

"They better not," Jackie said. "It wouldn't be fair, before any of the rest of us even got a chance to be in it."

"Yeah," said Billy. "My brother brought home this neat book about whales that he's crazy about, and I thought, Hey, I bet I could read that at Concord." He laughed. "I should have thought of it before. Now, somebody might say whales are smut."

"O.K., people," Ms. Plotkin said. "I know the school board meeting's on all of your minds. But we aren't going to talk about it this morning. We've been neglecting our workbooks for too long. Today I want to get back to participial clauses."

There was a groan. But Ms. Plotkin made us get out our workbooks and do a whole page of exercises. You had to make sentences using words they gave you. For 'although . . . still' I put, 'Although I have been worried about the school board meeting, I still have to admit I am eager to see how it turns out.' I nudged Rosemary and showed it to her. "Me, too," she whispered. "I'm crossing my fingers."

Maudie leaned over from the next row and dropped a note on my desk. "What are you going to wear tonight?" it said.

I hadn't thought about it. "Maybe a skirt?" I wrote back. "So no one thinks I'm a freak."

Maudie wrote another note. "I will too, then," it said. "And my velour shirt."

"Neat—I love that shirt," I wrote.

"Thanks!!!" Maudie wrote back in big letters. She was smiling. I realized I'd probably never paid her a compliment before.

"Kate and Maudie!" Ms. Plotkin said suddenly. "Is this note-writing necessary?"

We grinned sheepishly at each other. "Not exactly," I said.

"Well, then," she said, "let's get back to work."

Hastily, Maudie and I bent over our workbooks. Those participles took practically the whole hour. It was pretty boring. English is more interesting when it's about ideas.

"I hope I'll see most of you tonight at the school board meeting," Ms. Plotkin said when the bell finally rang. "We'll talk about it in class tomorrow."

Maudie and I gathered up our things. Ms. Plotkin came over and put an arm around each of us. "See you tonight," she said.

"Kate might make a speech," Maudie told her.

"Maudie! I didn't say I would—" I began.

"Oh, I think that would be wonderful, Kate," Ms. Plotkin interrupted. "People ought to hear how you kids feel about all this."

"Well," I said. "I don't know."

In the hall, I bopped Maudie. "Boy. Now you've got me in for it!"

"You don't *have* to do it," she said. "I hope you do, though. You'd be so *good*."

That's the thing about Maudie—she gives you confidence in yourself. Still, I didn't know how I could speak without getting all embarrassed.

And something that happened later in biology class really made me wonder. It happens that most of my friends aren't in that class. No one from English is. I sit at a table off to the side. Mr. Barnes was describing the digestive system of the human body and drawing a diagram of it on the blackboard. As soon as he got *near*

*124

the part about elimination some kids started snickering, and when he mentioned "bowels" half the room got hysterical. I began to feel myself blushing. I took out my notebook and concentrated on copying the diagram, shading in the large intestine very carefully. It's sort of an interesting shape, if you don't think about what it's for. I hated myself for being embarrassed but I just couldn't help it.

I sat there waiting for the end-of-school bell to ring. When it did I ran to my locker and got my things and hurried home. I didn't want to talk to anybody.

The *Crier* was on the porch when I got there. I took it into the kitchen and spread it out on the table with a sinking feeling in my stomach. I didn't know *what* would be in it.

Was I surprised. Instead of a bunch of angry letters, there was a whole page of sympathetic ones. And the first was from Aunt Lucy! I hadn't even realized she'd know what was going on, but I should have. They get the *Crier* at the nursing home, and Aunt Lucy always reads it. Lots of times she gives me her opinions on the news, or on Ann Landers. She loves it when Ann Landers scolds some reader.

Her letter to the editor was just terrific.

Having lived in Sussex for over a century, I believe I have earned the right to speak my mind when I get the urge. I got the urge yesterday, reading the Letters column, where some misguided folks complained about a book my great-grandniece, Kate Harris, read at

*125

Concord School, calling it "smut." I must tell you that Kate has read that very book to me and my friends at Shore Acres Nursing Home, and not one of us "senior citizens" was shocked by it—in fact, it delighted us all.

In my long life, I have witnessed many tragic events, among them five terrible wars, two hurricanes (in one of which the sea wall along Shore Road and nearly fifty lovely homes were demolished) and the deaths of many people near and dear to me. I have seen many puppies born, and many old dogs die. As a child, I tearfully buried four well-loved pets beneath the cedar tree beside my home on Turner Road.

Living through these events gives me some perspective. To me, life—all life, from the birth of living creatures to their death—is beautiful. Please accept an old lady's plea: Teach our little ones reverence for life! Let them see, as this book shows them, that every birth is natural and wonderful and a cause for joy.

And before we allow ourselves to get caught in useless dissension, let us remember that Sussex is our Home. We live here together, as neighbors and as friends. Let us stand together for the things that unite us, like the right of free expression granted to each one of us in our blessed Constitution.

My love to you all.
Lucy Colby Harris

What a letter! Aunt Lucy's about the smartest person I know. Her mind may sometimes go blank on little details, but when it comes to important things she's sharper than most people. I guess it's from living all those years.

I was sure her letter would calm people down. Mom said the same thing when she read it.

"That's just what we needed, Roy," she told Dad, "to bring people to their senses."

"Aunt Lucy's a remarkable woman," Dad said, smiling at me. "You take after her, Kate. You've got that old Harris spunk."

For some reason I almost cried when he said that. "What's for supper?" I asked, to cover up.

"Let's just warm up that split pea soup I made for Josh," Mom said. "That'll save time. We don't want to be late for the meeting."

"Where *is* Josh, anyway?" I asked. "He should be home by now."

"He'll be here any minute," Mom said. "He called the office to say he was studying late at the library."

I wondered if that meant he was with Denise. I hoped so. Maybe he'd talked things out with her. I wasn't all that crazy about Denise, but Josh did like her a lot. It would have been awful if they broke up over something to do with me.

Just then there was a stomping on the back steps and Josh came inside.

"Get a lot of studying done?" Dad asked him right away. My parents can be so innocent.

"Yeah." Josh gave me a private grin. He must have worked things out with Denise.

"Some people are fools for work," I said ironically, to let him know I understood.

Josh bopped me on the shoulder. "You've got it."

*127

We ate supper fast. The split pea soup was delicious. Mom had warmed up some corn bread to go with it. When we have a meal like that I can actually imagine becoming a vegetarian. If only fried clams and hamburgers didn't smell so good, I might.

chapter 16

* * *

THE HIGH SCHOOL parking lot was jammed, and the streets around it were full of cars. Dad had to drive two blocks away to find a space. We got out of the car and hurried back, hanging on to each other so we wouldn't slip on the icy sidewalk. The sky was that deep winter blue with millions of sparkly stars.

When we reached the auditorium door, Dad turned to me. "We're with you, Kate."

"Right," said Josh.

Mom just squeezed my arm without saying anything.

Then we went in.

The auditorium was packed. We stood in back, looking for a place to sit. It seemed as though everyone I knew—kids from school, relatives, neighbors, clients of my parents—was there, along with a lot of people I didn't know at all. The school board sat at a table on the stage. I saw Gerda and Mrs. Brooks in the front row, and Ms. Plotkin with Ms. Dwyer sitting behind them. Ms. Plotkin turned around and waved. She wasn't smiling.

Suddenly someone called "Roy!" in a booming voice. It was Mr. McConnell, with Mrs. McConnell beside him. Denise was there, too, hanging back.

Before I could say anything, Dad and Mom were heading right over. Josh poked me. "Go," he said tensely, and we followed them. He went over to Denise and left me standing alone behind Mom while she and Dad and Denise's parents made those loud, pointless remarks that adults always say in public places, the kind where nothing's funny but they laugh.

"Hi, there, Kate!" Mr. McConnell said suddenly, grabbing out for my hand and shaking it as though nothing had happened. "Say, we'd better grab some seats," he boomed out, and before I could stop Mom and Dad they trailed down the aisle after the McConnells. I followed, with Denise and Josh behind me. When our parents got to the empty row they bunched up and started arguing about who should go in first. Finally Mr. McConnell and Dad headed in, and then Mrs. McConnell and Mom. I went next so Josh could be with Denise. When we were all settled I scrunched down in my chair to be inconspicuous. I hate getting seated in public with everyone staring at you.

I poked Mom. "Why did we have to sit with *them?*" I whispered.

"Dad *likes* John McConnell," she whispered back. "They spent a lot of years together on the Planning Commission." She patted my hand. "You wouldn't want them to act unfriendly just because of this one thing."

In a way I would have. There *is* such a thing as family loyalty. Still, for Josh's sake it was good our parents weren't stupid about it like Romeo and Juliet's. I glanced over at him and Denise. Right in public, they were holding hands! I saw Mom nudge Mrs. McConnell and smile about it. Feeling sort of out of things, I began to look around for my friends. I saw Jackie and Rosemary and Christine sitting together a few rows in front of us, and Billy Taylor and Cal Berg behind them. I searched around for Steve Bader and finally saw him down in front with his parents and his older sister. I didn't see Maudie. The room was noisy. People were calling to each other and jumping up. I wondered which people had written the angry letters. Everyone there looked fairly pleasant, actually. It would be more convenient if mean people *looked* mean, so you could tell.

Then Maudie and her mother came in through the side door. I stood up and waved, and they waved back. Mom started waving at Mrs. Schmidt, but before she got too conspicuous about it, Maudie pointed to some seats a couple of rows in front of us, and the two of them headed down the aisle. I watched them squeeze into the row and sit down—right next to the Millers!

I bent over and caught Dad's eye. "The Millers!" I whispered.

"Lie low," Dad said comfortably. Dad really likes public meetings. In a way, I think he almost enjoys controversy. He probably should have been the President—except then Josh and I would have had to live in the White House. I don't think a kid would like that.

Maudie was looking around at me, saying something that I couldn't understand. Then I got it—she was mouthing "bubble gum."

I cracked up.

"Kate—settle down," Mom said, pressing my knee.

A man had begun to test the public address system. There was a sudden hush in the room. I tensed up, wondering if I would have the nerve to speak. My parka slid off my lap to the floor. When I bent over to pick it up, my bike lock clattered out of a pocket. People turned around. I scrunched down again and tried to look inconspicuous.

A woman got up from the board table and went to the mike. "Ladies and gentlemen," she said. "The topic that has brought us out on this cold night is an interschool reading project that was recently begun, involving Revere and Concord students. The board will vote later on whether the project should be continued. But first, we want to hear your feelings on this issue." She looked around the room. "Before we open the floor for discussion, I've asked two speakers to make presentations: Mr. John Staley, the principal of Revere School, and Mrs. Judith Bergen, parent of two Concord students."

Mr. Staley, looking as worried as usual, walked to

the microphone and fidgeted with it. Then he began to describe the project, going all the way back to the day last fall when Ms. Plotkin met Ms. Dwyer at the orientation for new teachers. Mr. Staley's an extremely dull speaker, but in a way that was good. It made the project sound more boring than dangerous.

Mrs. Bergen was another story. She had a loud voice which got even louder as she warmed up. According to her, Ms. Plotkin and Ms. Dwyer had made up a plot to teach impressionable children about sex. She held up a copy of *The Birthday Dog*, opened to the picture where the puppy gets born, to prove it. That wasn't fair! She should have read the whole book or not shown any of it.

"I'm the chairman of a group called Parents United for Decency," she said then. "We're asking the board to vote against this project or any other that undermines our children's morals!" She looked around the auditorium expectantly. But only a few people clapped.

"She didn't do so well with her sign-up sheet," Mom whispered, nudging me, as Mrs. Bergen sat down. "That's a relief!"

The woman from the board said, "And now, the floor is open to discussion." Right away, people began to jump up and shout for attention, arguing about who was first. Adults sometimes act worse than little kids.

But the discussion started out pretty well. The people who spoke first were all in favor of the project. Mrs. Bader talked seriously about "freedom to learn," and thanked the teachers for working so hard on the project. Another woman said that with all the good books children were exposed to, she didn't see how any one book could undermine their morals.

Then Mrs. Brooks jumped up. "And certainly not this one!" She put on her glasses and read two very enthusiastic reviews of *The Birthday Dog* all the way through. In her nice, grandmotherly way, she described how carefully she and Gerda choose library books. "We want every child to love reading," she finished, and everybody clapped.

I clapped too, but I was getting more and more nervous. Each time a speaker sat down I tried to work up the nerve to stand up. But I didn't know how to catch the board woman's attention, or what I'd say if she called on me. The room was stuffy and the bright lights made me dizzy. I wondered if I was going to faint.

Then a woman stood up and said, "My daughter Myra is in the first grade at Concord School, so I have first-hand knowledge—"

Myra! I tried to remember what she looked like.

"Sexual parts!" the woman went on. "They named them in front of those innocent children!"

How could she say that? She made it sound terrible. I felt so sorry for Myra.

"*What* parts?" somebody yelled from the back of the room. Some people laughed. I guess it was sort of an adult joke.

"The male and female *organs*," Mrs. James said furiously. "I won't say the words in mixed company."

*134

"*Spell* them!" the voice yelled. People laughed again. But I didn't think it was funny.

Mrs. James was red in the face. "You should be ashamed of yourselves, all of you!" she shouted. "Everyone who had anything to do with this project should be ashamed. You're corrupting little children!"

Mom was sitting on the edge of her seat. I suddenly realized she was about to stand up and defend me, and I didn't want her to. *I* could do it.

"I'm not ashamed!" I said, jumping up. I was surprised how loud my voice sounded.

People turned to look at me. The room got still.

"I'm Kate Harris," I went on defiantly. "I'm the one who read that book to the kids at Concord. I'm not ashamed of it. I think everybody in this room should read the whole thing before they criticize it. It's *good*. The kids really loved it. And it's not dirty. It's—" I searched for the right word. "It's educational!" I said.

I suddenly realized that everyone was staring at me—all those parents and kids and teachers—Gerda and Mrs. Brooks and Mr. Hofsteder, Mr. Staley, Steve Bader, everyone—and that I didn't mind. It was a relief to say what I thought.

But I realized that I didn't need to come out and say "penis" or anything in public. Why should I? It wouldn't be natural, the way it was with the kids.

"The words Mrs. James means," I said, "aren't even *in* the book. Some kids said them after I read it, but in an innocent way." In the blur of faces I made out Ms. Plotkin, smiling at me. "Anyway, I think it's good for kids to learn the right words," I said resolutely. "And not be embarrassed about them like us."

"Hear, hear!" someone shouted.

I wasn't finished. "I just want to say," I went on, "that I think kids have a right to learn things. That's what the project was for. I've already learned a lot, and I think I can help the little kids learn to read. It's a good project," I said, starting to choke up. "I hope it doesn't have to stop now." I sat down abruptly. My legs were shaking.

Mom squeezed my hand. People smiled. And there was this big wave of applause.

I sank back in my seat, exhausted. It's hard work to speak in public.

Just then, somebody tapped my shoulder. For a second I didn't recognize Dr. Klingman without his white coat. "That was a fine speech," he said, smiling.

"Oh thanks," I said, hoping my teeth had looked clean while I was talking.

It seemed as though the whole discussion changed after that. Ms. Dwyer and Ms. Plotkin announced parent meetings about the project. And Gerda invited everyone to come to a book-and-coffee hour at the library on Wednesdays. She said they'd pick a different book to discuss each week, and everyone who read it through was welcome.

"That's a good move," Dad said, clapping. I noticed that the McConnells were clapping, too.

Then the woman from the school board got up. "Before the board votes, I want to take a minute to

136

read from a letter in today's *Crier*. It's from Aunt Lucy Harris, our oldest citizen." She peered through her glasses. "Sussex is our home," she read. "We live here together as neighbors and as friends. Let us stand together for the things that unite us."

The room broke into applause. Aunt Lucy would have been pleased.

"The question before the board is whether the interschool project should continue," the woman said then, and began to call out names. The vote went very fast. The first five board members said "Aye," the next one said "Nay," and the last person said "Aye" again. That was it! I could hardly believe it. I turned around to look at Maudie. She was waving happily. "We won!" I shouted at her, even though she couldn't hear me through the noise. "We won!" I said to Mom.

Mom hugged me, and so did Dad. Josh whapped me on the back a few times and Denise said "Congratulations." Then Mr. McConnell reached over and grabbed my hand. "You were a very convincing speaker," he said. "She certainly was," Mrs. McConnell chimed in. Maybe I actually *had* convinced them. Josh and Denise should be pretty grateful to me. I turned to give them a knowing look, but they had already started down the aisle. It was jammed with people talking excitedly.

"Let's go," Dad said, "or we'll never get out of here."

I started along the row, just as Ms. Plotkin came rushing down the next one. She leaned over and hugged me. "I was so proud of you!" she said. "Wasn't she marvelous?" she asked Mom and Dad, who were beaming.

Over her head, I saw Mrs. James talking grimly to Mrs. Bergen. I wondered how they felt.

Someone tapped my shoulder. "Kate? I'm Marge Robbins. I just wanted to introduce myself and congratulate you, and tell you that Alexandra can't wait till you come to baby-sit."

"Oh, I can't wait, either!" I said. It was good to meet Mrs. Robbins here—now I wouldn't feel so shy when I went to her house.

We had pushed out to the aisle. People were still milling about in little clumps. I saw Maudie standing with Jackie and Billy and Rosemary across the room.

"Maudie!"

We made our way toward each other. "You were terrific!" Maudie said, hugging me. "I *told* you you would be."

"Yeah," I said happily, as the other kids crowded over. Then I looked up and saw Dad pointing to the door. "I have to go—see you all tomorrow." I hurried to the back and went out the door. Mom and Dad were already halfway down the block. I shivered in the cold air. Suddenly I noticed two people standing near a pine tree. It was Josh kissing Denise!

What a night. Pretending I hadn't seen anything, I ran down the sidewalk after Mom and Dad. Josh caught up to me just before I got to the car. He looked sheepish.

"Where were you, Josh?" Mom asked. "I was looking all over for you."

"I got caught in the crowd," Josh said innocently. I poked him, so he'd know I knew. He poked me back, grinning.

Dad drove slowly over the snow-packed street. I leaned back against my seat, thinking about the meeting. Something kept bothering me. "The thing is," I said aloud, "the board's vote probably didn't change Mrs. Bergen's mind. I wish—" I reached over the seat to touch Mom's shoulder. "You know. I wish people agreed more. I wish they agreed with *me*."

Mom patted my hand. "I know how you feel."

"People will always disagree," Dad said. "That's life. But I think this meeting has cleared the air. Parents know more about the project now. And it was clear that only a few people were upset. They had their say, but the majority opinion went against them. And that's democracy."

"But still. The majority wins and the minority doesn't like it." In my mind, I saw Mrs. James waving her arms wildly. My thoughts kept jumping around, I was so tired.

"I wouldn't like it if *I* was the minority and Mrs. Bergen's side won," I said.

"At least, most people there were for freedom of speech," Josh said.

"Yeah," I persisted. "But what if one person's freedom of speech bumps into someone else's right not to hear something." Oh, man, it was complicated.

"What about when Mrs. Bergen uses *her* free speech to try to stop me from having mine?"

"There aren't any easy answers, Katie," Dad said, turning into our driveway. "People just have to keep trying to work out solutions the best they can. They won't ever be perfect."

"Yeah," I said. I wished there *were* easy answers, and perfect solutions. That would save an awful lot of effort. Anyway, at least the project was safe. Soon I'd see all the kids again.

All of a sudden I could hardly wait to crawl into bed. I was exhausted. *Democracy* is exhausting.

chapter 17

✳ ✳ ✳

"YOU KNOW what I think?" Maudie asked seriously.

It was a few weeks later. We were walking to my house from the Concord library. Maudie was coming for supper. There was a fantastic sunset across the sky that made the dirty snow on the sidewalks look pink.

"What?" I jumped across a slushy puddle.

"I think the project was worth all the trouble," Maudie said.

"Oh, so do I!" I shifted my book bag to the other shoulder. "I feel so much more, you know, *experienced* now."

We'd been having an after-school workshop on issues in children's books with Mrs. Brooks and Ms. Dwyer. Steve and Rosemary and Jackie had been there, too. They were in the project now, and other kids from our English class were on the waiting list. All of a sudden it seemed as though everyone wanted to get into it.

"It's funny how the more you learn, the more complicated things get," Maudie said. "Like, I used to think writing books for little kids would be a cinch."

"I used to think *reading* them would be! Boy, were we innocent back then."

"We learned the hard way." Maudie pulled up her hood.

"So did some other people," I said. "Mrs. Bergen learned she couldn't push this whole town around."

"Not that she and her group won't keep trying," Maudie said.

"I know. But even some of *them* are learning. Mom told me that Mrs. James came to Gerda's last discussion group and actually said something good about one of the books."

Mom had been to all Gerda's meetings. She was getting very interested in teen-age novels. In a way, I sort of hated to have her read them. It spoils your privacy when parents begin to think they *understand* you. Mom kept recommending books to Josh that he probably wished she didn't even know about. The thing is, you can't censor your mother's reading.

"Does Mrs. Bergen come to those meetings?" Maudie asked.

"I don't think so. We should just be grateful that Parents for Decency has faded away for now."

"That's true," Maudie said. "But you never know when they'll find a new dirty book. Last night I really got scared when I saw a table outside the A & P. But then you know what it was? People selling chances for a color TV!"

"Yeah, and Mr. Miller called up the other day, but all he wanted was for Dad to check out a radiator!"

"And so," Maudie began in a fake announcer's voice, "at least for now, life returns to normal in the sleepy little seacoast town of Sussex, Mass., and the inhabitants take up their ordinary lives once more—"

"Don't forget our budding careers!" I interrupted.

Maudie and I were both baby-sitters now. I'd been to Alexandra's three different times and Maudie'd sat for Simon twice. And I was hoping to baby-sit a real baby soon. The Liebermans bought the Shore Road house from my parents after all, and their baby was due any day. Naturally, Mom had already boasted about what a good sitter I was.

Maudie started up with her announcer's voice again. "And a hint of romance hovers in the air as Kate Harris blushingly admits that Steve Bader's starting to be her boy friend."

"Maudie! He is *not!* Just because I went to his house a couple of times—" I poked her arm.

"Three times, at least," Maudie teased.

"Maudie, honestly—you sound like Mom!"

It was true. The first time I went to Steve's, Mom kept saying it was wonderful that I'd made a new friend. But the other day, she looked sort of worried and told me I shouldn't bother the Baders all the time. I think she's getting ideas from all those books she's reading about what Steve and I might be doing.

Actually, we don't do anything except talk and eat and maybe study, but I don't always want to give her instant replays. Now I can really sympathize with Josh.

We had turned into my block when a car slowed down in the street beside us. We looked around. A little boy in the back seat was waving wildly at us through the window.

"It's Richard," Maudie said. "Hi, Richard!"

Richard's mother smiled at us from the driver's seat. Then she gave a little honk and drove off.

"It's neat how the kids get so excited whenever they see us," I said. It happened all the time. Wherever I went, it seemed as though a kid from Ms. Dwyer's class would run up and hug me. It made me feel kind of famous.

We waved at the car till it disappeared.

"Bye!" Maudie shouted after it. Her hood had slipped down and her face was pink from the wind. She has such a friendly face.

"Come on!" I said suddenly, putting my arm over her shoulders. "I'm starving."

Then, matching steps, we went up my front walk together.

BETTY MILES is well known for her honest and engaging novels, including THE REAL ME, JUST THE BEGINNING, ALL IT TAKES IS PRACTICE, LOOKING ON and THE TROUBLE WITH THIRTEEN (all Knopf), as well as for her many books for younger readers.

A graduate of Antioch College, Betty Miles has taught children's literature and has been on the staff of the publications division at Bank Street College of Education. She lives in Rockland County, New York.